AF226068

The Unveiling

Dedicated to my treasures:

Joni, Ray, Heather, Lauren, Conor, Lincoln, Tyler, Carter, Annabella and Gerry

Chapter 1

Bre stood in the doorway, her heart pounding. Someone was in her house, and it wasn't the first time.

Her eyes searched the living room. Everything seemed to be in order, but the silent alarm told her otherwise. She moved forward, her eyes looking for anything that would give evidence of the intruder. Slowly, room by room she inched her way until she stood outside her office. Silently she opened the door. Her chair had been pushed back from the desk and turned slightly toward the door. Her eyes searched the room, glancing up she noticed the light was on. "That light was off when I left, and I always push my chair in." Her mind was racing. What was going on? Life was no longer the same. Even as the thought surfaced, Bre realized it had never been normal.

Bre considered her childhood to have been safe, happy, and stable. She was twelve when her mom and dad had decided to tell her she was adopted. Her parents had been married ten years without children and had decided to try other options. They had barely received the news that there would be a child born in seven months, and they had been chosen by the birth mother to raise her child when her adoptive mother realized she was pregnant. Elated by the news, they paused to consider having two at once. After prayer, her parents decided to continue with the adoption. Having two only two months apart would be a handful, but they rejoiced at the blessing.

It was several months later when news reached them that the birth mother was carrying twins. The announcement came as a shock. Three children would be impossible for them to handle, not to mention the cost. After much prayer, an agreement with the birth mother brought about a solution. They would adopt one, and the other twin would go to another couple. Throughout the years Bre wondered what her biological sister looked like, and what she had done with her life. Was she raised in a good home like herself? Her brother who arrived two months after her entrance had always been a blessing. Close from the beginning, she and Michael remained close even after the tragic accident that claimed the lives of both her mother and father. They would meet for lunch to comfort one another and to encourage one another with memories that caused both to laugh, though both left with a deep longing for what was.

Perhaps that was the reason Bre had sought a private investigator to search for her birth mother and sister. She had little information, as her adoptive parents shared little. She knew the day and year she was born along with the name of the hospital. She wasn't told the city or state but that she was a twin and the other child was a girl. The investigation had been going on for a few months and, although her mind drifted to it occasionally, the awareness that someone was entering her house took priority.

How were they getting in? There was no sign of forced entry. How would they know the code for the security device, and why was her computer always gone through? The first time the machine was up after she had noticed the silent alarm system, she found "file corrupted" flashing across her screen. Her mind raced now as she sat at her desk. The computer was up in seconds, and again, the "file corrupted" flashed. Bre was not advanced in computers, she knew how to bring them up to check her mail, file her clients' information, along with their notes to keep on record. Could that be it? Was someone she was counseling in trouble with the government? Her mind raced to the different movies she had seen, spies and individuals least expected. "Oh God, make some sense of this, please."

Suddenly, the house that had been a gift from her parents seemed too large and too watched. She walked outside hoping it would clear her head. As she walked towards the pool, she glanced back at the house. It was impressive, one of many in the gated community that only those with high income would attempt to own. Unaware of her parents' wealth, it took their death before she would grasp the accurate measure. Her father had owned several pharmaceutical companies which provided well by the time she had reached her teens. She had received her education at the best colleges, both in undergraduate and graduate degrees. She knew when dealing with individuals minds and emotions she wanted the best available. Not willing to accept the standard teachings from different psychotherapists who failed to consider the spiritual. She recognized that some, like Freud, emphasized the significance of the unconscious processes to determine behavior and affect personality.

Still, after several years of working closely with the prosecutors and dealing with cases she'd rather forget; she decided to start her practice. She loved the freedom of choosing her clients and determining her daily schedule. The inheritance from her parents came as a shock, with hundreds of millions provided for both her and her brother. She would never have to work again if that was her wish. Still to do nothing was to waste one's life to which she was opposed. Her mind drifted to her biological sister. Did she have a good education, and was she able to afford what she needed? The ache that had begun with the death of her parents had grown to include her twin. She physically experienced a deep longing that only the encounter would quench.

A movement caught her eye, and she focused on her new neighbor walking his dog. He had moved in a few months earlier and appeared to be single, except for his dog which he walked daily if not several times a day. She had met him once at a nearby drugstore where she had run in to pick up some photos. She had noticed him immediately, not associating him as her neighbor just an attractive man. He stood six feet, two or three inches tall, dark hair cut close, yet long enough in front to cause him to appear boyish. His physical build reversed that opinion. His chest and arms gave evidence to a regular weight building routine, and she would guess him to be of Spanish descent. A ready smile revealed even white teeth and a square jaw that gave the appearance of an aristocrat.

Bre had smiled, nodded, and hurried along. He appeared undaunted and stood until she turned to leave. He then stepped in front of her, smiling with a look of amusement playing on his face. "I believe we are neighbors ,and in our busy world I felt I should seize this chance to introduce myself." Bre had stopped abruptly staring into the stranger's handsome face. His arrival would have gone unnoticed if she had been working away from her home, but with her office now in her home, she had observed the moving vans that arrived to unload his furniture.

They had talked briefly and parted. Now Bre watched her neighbor glanced in her direction, smile, and began to walk towards her. Bre's heart quickened, "Stop it! You're acting like a teenager."

Carlos' smile widened as he drew near. "You look preoccupied while doing nothing." His comment irritated her.

"How would you know?" Her answer sounded harsh to her ears and came across stronger than she had intended. He paused, tilted his head slightly, and continued to smile. "Sorry, that was out of order. My mind was preoccupied, and I was doing nothing." Carlos' laugh was contagious, one that drew others in and caused Bre to laugh.

Suddenly, it felt good to laugh. It had been a long time. "Would you like something to drink? I was going to take a break and relax for a while." Carlos' eyes studied every inch of her face. She was lovely; a beauty really; and unmarried. It seemed odd. She was well educated, that was obvious with a grace when she walked and a slow consideration when she spoke. Standing five feet seven, she couldn't have weighed more than a hundred and twenty pounds, auburn hair that fell around her shoulders, an oval face, and flashing green eyes that would have turned anyone's head, yet he had never seen her with anyone.

"I would love that, whatever you're having." She motioned to several patio sets that surrounded the pool. He sat watching her walk towards the house. "I need to know her." His desire had been awakened earlier with their encounter at the drugstore, and he had made a point to walk his dog by her house each day, in hopes that he might be able to talk with her. Today he had been rewarded, and he intended to gain as much insight as he could for as long as he could.

"What are you doing?" Bre asked herself while walking back into her house. When entering her home, a sadness suddenly swept over her so strong that she leaned against the wall. The loneliness that had become her constant companion threatened to overtake her. "Oh, God. Oh, God." Tears streamed down her face, would this sadness ever leave? The minutes ticked by, then slowly the feelings lifted. She glanced out her patio door. Carlos would be wondering. A strange peace filled her, and she quickly filled two glasses with tea. Glancing at her reflection in the mirror, she erased evidence of a tear-stained face and promptly began walking to meet Carlos.

Carlos had sat several minutes, before raising the umbrella. The California sun could be scorching, and although they were only a few miles from the ocean which provided a welcome breeze, one learned to protect oneself from the sun. Not that it was a concern for him. Being raised in Brazil, he was used to the sun. His family owned several coffee plantations that had continued for several generations. He had been in charge of marketing globally and had moved to California to establish a new base within the United States. At the age of thirty, he worked and knew every aspect of coffee. His college degrees in marketing had benefited the family business and placed him as CEO, with his sister overseeing the plantations in Brazil. His life was good and had been full amid his family, but here in the States he was, for the first time in his life, experiencing loneliness.

Bre's appearance brought a smile to his face. She placed the glasses on the table, along with some sweeteners, as she apologized for taking so long. Carlos' eyes studied her face. Her eyes shone brightly; too bright; as if she had been crying. "Are you alright?" The question caught Bre off guard, and before she knew it, she began telling him of her parents' death, stopping short of her search for her biological sister and the mysterious invasion of her home.

Carlos listened quietly, nodding slowly. Bre paused. What was she doing? He was a perfect stranger and yet she knew that talking helps to bring healing. She had seen it with her clients, and now she was experiencing it. After a few moments of silence, Carlos began to share of his home life in Brazil. His family, the business, and the death of his brother as a young teen; who was a drowning victim on an outing. At the time Carlos cursed himself for not having been with him, then later he questioned if he had been there and would have been unable to save him against the current; would he have been able to handle that guilt? After many years he remembered him with a smile, thinking of his humor, his practical jokes; and wishing, yes, wishing things had been different, just as Bre was now.

As he shared that revelation with her, Bre felt they were somehow connected, if by nothing else but the sadness of their loss. She looked at him and felt a closeness. Strange, hours ago he meant nothing, but as he reached for her hand and gently squeezed it, she didn't pull back. Together they stared into one another's eyes. Bre's heart began to quicken, and she wondered if Carlos was experiencing the same thing. Both smiled at one another. Without verbalizing it, both knew something had shifted in their spirits, in their emotions, and their lives.

"What are you doing this evening?" Without waiting for an answer Carlos continued, "I was thinking, perhaps you would join me for dinner as I'm new to the area and have grown tired of my cooking. The restaurant of your choice." After a slight pause, he whispered, "Please."

His voice brought a smile to her face and, after a moment, she replied, "I had no plans and would love to join you. Could you pick me up at six?"

Carlos stood and slowly lifted her hand to kiss it. "I look forward to seeing you at six." He nodded slightly, motioning to his dog and began to walk towards his house. A backward glance caused Bre to laugh out loud. Picking up her glasses, she headed back to the house. Her only thought was on what she would wear for that night and for the first time in a long time, she was glad to be alive.

Chapter 2

Michael watched his sister as she approached his table at their favorite restaurant. There was a bounce to her step, and a smile on her face he hadn't seen for a long time. "I'm sorry I'm running late. The traffic was horrific." Bre's face flushed. The truth was, Carlos had stopped by on his way out of town on business, and it was hard to tear herself away, realizing he would be absent for days. The past few weeks had taken her by surprise. One dinner led to the next with conversations that ran deep into the night. Before she knew it, Carlos was the first thought upon waking and the last before going to sleep. "You need to slow down," she told herself, but Carlos gave no inclination of wanting that to happen. He would call early in the morning to ask how she slept and what were her plans for the day. His words caressed her, causing a deep longing to be near him. She had never felt like this before.

Her schooling through the years demanded much of her time, and although there had been dates during high school and college, there was no one that took her breath away or caused her to long for his next call. Carlos appeared to feel the same, staring deep into her eyes, his hand caressing hers, or his fingers trailing up and down her arms. It took weeks before he had kissed her and she felt she would scream if he hadn't finally drawn her to him with a kiss so deep and long it took her breath away.

Remembering the moment, the way both of them gazed into each other's eyes, their rapid breathing revealing their emotions. It was Carlos who stepped back, drew a deep breath and slowly released a soft whistle. "We must be patient. We must do this right." She wasn't bold enough to ask for an explanation. She had just smiled and nodded while walking into his arms. He had held her close, and she could feel the rapid beating of his heart,

"I would like you to meet my family. Would you be willing to do that?" The question caught her by surprise and caused her heart to skip a beat.

"I would like that very much."

Carlos had informed her on his way out of town that his mother and father were planning on visiting the following month. Bre's mind was racing with visions of the future when she arrived at the restaurant to meet Michael.

After placing their order, Michael smiled at Bre. "You have the look of love, what has happened?" Bre smiled at her brother and then began to relate what had transpired the last few weeks. Michael listened attentively weighing each word. Bre was a good judge of character and was able to zero in on personality faults quickly. It was a valued asset in her profession, and Michael trusted her opinion. By the time they had finished their meal, he was able to say, "I'd like to meet Carlos let me know when it works for the two of you."

Bre reached for her brother's hand. "I think you'll like him." She received a smile that assured her he would.

Michael left Bre relieved. He had watched his sister bury herself in work since the death of their parents. After two years, he was beginning to wonder what it would take to give her a vision for the future. It was different for him. He had Deborah, and though the accident had rocked his world, she enabled him to refocus while giving him the space to grieve. His mind drifted back to their wedding, only months before the accident. How strange, one moment his world was full of life, then the next death.

It had been two years. Two years and still not a day passed that he didn't wish with deep longing for just one more chance to tell the two most important people, how much he loved them and how much he had treasured them. He remembered Bre's bright smile and the joy in her face. She was beginning to live again. Yes, having someone made the difference. If Carlos was the one bringing about this change, then he was all for him.

Bre returned home relaxed and joyful. Her time with her brother focused on her future not reflecting on the past. Her world had been so wrapped up in the relationship with Carlos; she had forgotten about the search for her sister and mother until she brought up her laptop. The

RTF investigation had sent a "call immediately" as subject and a small note informing Bre that they had located her sister.

Bre sat staring at the e-mail, she hadn't mentioned anything to Carlos. "What am I thinking?" She hadn't mentioned anything to Michael either and he needs to know all that's been going on. Bre reflected, "It would be interesting to know if her life was normal or was she also experiencing the strange happenings.

Bre had went for several weeks and had not found her home security disabled. Then yesterday, she had returned from an appointment, and as she walked from her car to the door, she heard the security device sounding off. She opened her door to hear, "Beep! Beep! Beep!" but the security panel showed 14-13-12 counting down. In an instant, she understood what had happened. Someone had been in her home and saw her drive into the garage. They set the alarm, but she had gotten in before it counted from 60-0. If it had reached 0 when she entered, it would have begun as if no one had been there, from 60-down. Now she wondered how many times someone had been in her home and just set the alarm before she walked in. Where had they gone, how could they have gotten away so quickly? The thought caused her to draw in a deep breath as she reached for the phone to make the call to the agency.

She waited until Randal Franklin answered, to identify herself. "Fortunately, the hospital was in the same state, or we could have looked for months. All births records are in separate records on a disk. Fortunately, you're young enough; we were able to locate it fairly easy. Paper records are on file in a separate building."

Bre held her breath. "My sister, do you know where she is?"

Randal answered affirmatively. "We had to use the excuse of a medical emergency to persuade an employee to give the information - plus we gave a nice handshake." Randal chuckled on the other end. Bre sat for a second her mind not taking in what was said. "I don't understand."

Randal stated slowly, "The Privacy Act. It forbids the release of any information. The employee felt, in case of a life or death situation, it was worth releasing it."

Bre shook her head. "You said it was a matter of life or death?"

Randle was silent for a few moments then replied, "I lied, and it worked. Your sister lives two towns over from you, less than thirty miles away."

Bre spoke in a whisper, "What else do you know?" as she held her breath.

"Well let's see, raised in a middle-income household, with good parents, both still alive. She's a social worker who works with the court system."

Bre sat stunned. "What?" Bre spoke without realizing it "I work with the court system. What's her name?"

"Bethany Reynolds. She's 24, not married and lives in a townhouse at 'The Villas.' I'll send you the information. Do you still want me to continue the search for your birth mother?"

 Bre's mind was racing. "Yes please." She quickly hung up and began to walk the floor, a habit she'd picked up in college that helped her stay awake when studying for tests.

Bethany Reynolds, she knew the name but was having trouble recalling the face. She had worked with several case workers. Turning to her computer, she brought up the name and profile on her. Instantly she was looking at someone so familiar it amazed her that she hadn't seen the resemblances before. Same eyes, same turned up nose, only Bethany hair was blonde, and it was cut chin length to shape her oval face. If it was not colored and the same style, the likeness would be apparent.

"I kept all my records." Bre walked over to her file cabinet and began the search. Before long, she was staring at three different files with history and follow up from Bethany Reynolds. "I knew I recognized that name, but did I talk with her on the phone or just pass her at the courthouse?" She scanned the material. Billy Martin, she had just received something from the court system on him.

After walking the floor for half an hour, Bre made the call. "Could we meet to discuss a case?" Bethany was friendly but professional. The meeting was set for Friday, three days away. Bre's mind was racing. "I should talk with Michael." Carlos was gone, and suddenly she needed to talk things out. "Oh God," she wondered, "am I right in doing this?" She immediately felt, "Yes!" It felt solid in her mind, but Michael would have to know. She made the call. "I know we just met but something has come up and I just need to hear your thoughts."

Michael laughed. "Come tonight for dinner."

Bre hesitated. "Is Debora okay with such short notice?"

Michael laughed. "I'll bring home Chinese. She loves to see you. It's not often enough." Bre hung up feeling relief.

The afternoon passed by quickly, and Bre arrived at Michael's with dessert from her favorite bakery. True to his word, Michael had the counter lined with a Chinese buffet, and Deborah busied herself setting the table. The dinner had passed pleasantly and when Deborah excused herself, Michael and Bre made their way to the patio overlooking the pool. Bre began talking immediately, barely stopping for air. Michael looked surprised, then sat back quietly until Bre finished. At the last moment, Bre started to tell of her home invasion, the security system disarmed, and her coming in to hear the beeping counting down.

Michael sat up straight, his attention at full alert. "I'll have someone over tomorrow, if possible to install cameras, and I assure you, no one will be able to uninstall them." His anger was apparent, but something else was also surfacing. You could see fear for his sister written on his face. "I'll have the area patrolled."

Bre looked at her brother "Michael; It's a gated community."

Michael sat back and stared at Bre. "Well, someone is getting through the gate then. If I have to hire someone to stand guard in front and back of your house for three eight-hour shifts, then I'll do it!"

Bre looked at her brother. She knew him well. He didn't waste words. "I hadn't thought of that." Bre whispered, "Why hadn't I thought of that?" Michael was writing on a note pad he had carried in his front pocket, and Bre spoke out what she was thinking. "I don't know what I would have in my house that would interest anyone."

Michael stood. "Bre, you should do what you feel you need to do regarding your sister and birth mother, but I'm taking care of the intruder. You need to spend the night here." It was a statement of fact, not a question.

Bre looked at Michael. "Spend the night? Spend the night," Bre repeated. "Really?" Michael would have it no other way.

Several hours later, Bre closed her eyes to sleep in one of the extra bedrooms and woke the next morning when the alarm went off, realizing that she had slept better than she had in months. The reality of the intruder affecting her life began to become apparent to her. Without realizing it, she had slept for months half conscious. Carlos had relieved some of the stress in the excitement of the relationship, but her subconscious was still on high alert. Last night she was able to let her guard down, and it showed. She slept like a rock.

Michael wasted no time in carrying out his plan. By the next afternoon someone was there setting up cameras in every room - hallways and basement included. The outside, front, and back entrances were surveilled; along with the pool and surrounding area. Michael insisted on the footage being stored not only on the premises but also sent to another location away from the house, so there were two copies of all. He then interviewed the men, retired police officers, to run security. Bre allowed him to oversee everything, knowing he had her best interest at heart.

By the time Friday arrived Bre was able to leave home knowing every area: front, back, inside and out was covered.

Chapter 3

Bre arrived ten minutes early for her appointment with Bethany. It wasn't that she was ever late for any of her interviews, but after changing her clothes six times, it surprised her she made it on time. "It's important that I make a good first impression." She went from a tailored suit to a soft blouse and skirt. Finally, settling on a soft pale pink blouse, and white trousers, with white sling back heels. She grabbed a white clutch purse to finish the look. Then she debated, "Do I wear my hair up or down - curled or straight?" She finally settled on keeping it down, but with a light curl.

She sat impatiently waiting in the reception area; her foot tapped continually. Hearing her name called, she jumped then stood with a smile. Bethany stood before her. Bre stepped forward with her hand stretched out. "Good morning, thank you for seeing me on such short notice".

 Bethany smiled. "Not at all. Please come in." Her office was nice with a large window behind her desk that revealed the city at its best. Seven stories high, all you could see was the other skyscrapers and none of what littered the streets below. "Please have a seat. How can I help you?" Pleasant but professional, "Good," Bre thought. She had prepared herself on what she could ask regarding Billy, which was why she was supposed to be visiting.

In a short time, they had an agreement regarding the client, and Bre sat debating what her next move was. Suddenly, she decided to lay her cards on the table. Taking a deep breath, Bre smiled and stated, "There was another reason I wanted to see you. I have strong reasons to believe that we are biological sisters; twins from our birth mother." Bethany's eyes widened, her lips parted, and she sat silently while her eyes examined Bre. Suddenly, the similarities between the two became very apparent.

Bethany reached for her phone and asked her receptionist to cancel all her afternoon appointments.   "Tell me what you know," Bethany said as she sat back in her chair.

Bre starting by asking, "Were you aware you were adopted?"

"I was, I haven't pursued any information as my adoptive parents are living and I didn't want to offend them." Bethany answered, and then asked, "How long have you known I was your sister?"

Bre looked at her sister in the eyes - the same eyes that stared back at her each time she looked in the mirror. "I learned Tuesday of this week. A lot has happened this week." Bre reflected on Michael and all that had transpired at her house.

Both remained silent for several minutes then Bethany asked, "Have you learned the whereabouts of our mother?"

Bre shared what she had learned from the investigator, finishing with, "The search continues." The statement sounded strange even to her ears and wondered if it was the same to Bethany. Bre looked at her sister." How would you like to continue? I want to get to know you, know about you, and have a relationship with you, but I will accept whatever you decide." Bre held her breath.

Bethany smiled. "I'm an only child, and I would like that very much. Would you like to start with lunch?"

Over chicken salad, Texas toast and iced tea, each shared their highlights, accomplishments, and heartbreaks. Bre shared the profound loss she felt with her adoptive parents' deaths and of her joy at meeting Carlos. After debating for a few minutes, she shared about the strange incidents regarding her home and silent security alarm.

Bethany sat up straight upon hearing that. "That's strange." she replied, "Even stranger because I've had the same thing happen to me. I thought it had stopped, but maybe it hasn't. Maybe they have just become wise so I am unaware when I come in."

Bre stared at her sister. For both of them to be experiencing the same intrusion was clear this was no coincidence. No, someone was looking for something, but what? And how would anyone know they were sisters, as Bre had just learned that herself. They sat silent for several minutes, then Bre began to share what Michael had done to secure her home.

Bethany nodded. "When did your home invasion start?"

Bre stopped to consider the question. "After I started the investigation for you and Mom, two months ago."

Bethany looked at her. "It's been six weeks for me. I've noticed nothing different the last two weeks but then, again, as you've stated, they may have just gotten wiser." Both sat studying each other. It was obvious it had something to do with their search for each other and their mother. "Do you think she's alive - our biological mother?" Bethany asked.

Bre answered. "Something tells me she is, because someone, or ones are very interested in the same question."

Bre and Bethany parted with plans to meet Sunday evening for dinner. Bethany said she was going to share with her parents her meeting with Bre, in hopes that they would share any other information they might have regarding their birth mother.

Bre drove straight to Michael's office. As the head prosecutor, she hoped he might have some insight from his past cases. As luck would have it, Michael had just finished with his last interview and was able to take time to hear his sister. She received the same reaction from him as she had from Bethany regarding the intruder.

"Bre, when did this start?" Bre studied Michael's face.

"That's funny. It was the same question Bethany had asked. The answer is, not long after I began the search for Bethany and my birth mother. "Bre looked deep into Michael's eyes "Why? There's a connection isn't there?"

Michael silently nodded his head. "I can't believe it's the Franklin investigation. I've used them and recommended them numerous times. Still..." He sat tapping his pen then jotted down a few notes. "Let me have him checked out and see what I can find out. I'll get back with you as soon as I hear anything." As Bre stood to leave, Michael asked, "Are you feeling safe at home?"

Bre smiled. She felt sorry for the men posted all night in the front and back of her home, but yes, she was feeling safe. After a quick hug and a thank you, Bre left.

Carlos should be home tomorrow. She was anxious to see him, but so much had happened, she wasn't sure where to begin. The day passed slowly. Finally, Bre saw Carlos' BMW pull into her driveway. She held on to the door to keep from running out to see him, and counted to ten before she opened the door. Carlos stood leaning against the pillar a smile played at his lips. Bre stood still, suddenly at a loss for words. She could feel the heat rising from her neck. His smile widened, revealing white teeth.

Suddenly, with a deep laugh, Carlos enveloped her in his arms with a kiss so passionate it left Bre weak and clinging. Just as she opened her eyes, she saw Wayne walking quickly towards her, his hand in his pocket. She had forgotten the security Michael had set in place. Moving swiftly, Bre raised her hand to stop Wayne. Then reconsidering, she called Wayne over to introduce him to Carlos. Carlos was cordial but glanced at Bre, questioning. Bre smiled and led him inside.

"What was that all about?" he asked.

Bre drew Carlos into the kitchen, handing him a glass of tea. "How tired are you and how much time do you have?"

Carlos studied Bre's face. "I have all the time you need."

Bre drew Carlos to the couch and slowly began to share what all had taken place this past week. She told him about the investigation that led to finding her sister, the invasion into her house and discovering that her sister had also experienced the same thing.

Carlos drew Bre to him. "What do you make of it?"

Bre glanced out the window. "I live in a gated community, no one is even able to get in unless they have the code, yet they are, and not only my house, but my sister's. What do I make of it?" Bre turned to look at

Carlos. "I'd say someone is very interested in knowing about us but why? I'm not sure, but knowing Michael, it's just a matter of time before it is found out."

Carlos sat quietly and then turned to Bre. "Are your phones listened into?" Bre stared at him as if he was an alien.

"My phones?" The thought never entered her mind. "My phones?" she repeated. "I've never considered it."

Carlos took her hand in his. "Someone has been assigned to you and for a reason. They will use whatever is necessary to accomplish their aim. Now we need to discover who they are and what their aim is." Bre made a mental note to get another cell in a name other than her own.

Chapter 4

Carlos stayed until late talking and trying to reassure Bre, but when he left, she had difficulty sleeping. "What in the world is going on and how did all this start?" finally exhausted, she slept.

When she woke, she remembered her dinner with Bethany. The day passed quickly, and before she knew it, she was being seated across from her sister who was smiling at her. "How was your week?"

Bre hesitated to reply, "A lot has happened." Bre looked at her sister who was so like her. So much had happened, she had to stop and rethink what all she had already shared.

Bethany studied Bre's face. "Have there been more intrusions?"

Bre nodded. "But it's different than the past." She then stopped maybe it wasn't different. Perhaps that's the way it had always been, only now, there was a camera, but there was no physical manifestation. Bre told of what Carlos had said, finishing with his comment regarding her phone.

Suddenly Bethany's face changed. Bre knew before she asked. "You think someone's on your phone?"

Bethany nodded. "Someone is, and the telephone company can't explain it."

She leaned forward. "A few weeks ago, the phone in the bedroom rang. I glanced at the number. It wasn't familiar, so I let it ring. Just as the answering machine picked up, another line came in. I heard a voice answer "Darrel speaking" then the person calling spoke, "Hey Darrel, I'm in town." Then it faded out. I called the telephone company, who sent someone out. He listened to it, shook his head and asked to hear it again. His words were, "I'm confused." He checked the line and came back to hand me his card. He said, "Don't call the phone company; if it happens again, call me. I can't say I've solved your problem, as I can't figure out how it happened. I've worked here for years, and I've never had that happen. I went over my head to ask and heard " it wasn't possible." Bethany looked at Bre. He said, "I told them I heard it and they said it's not possible." He replied, "I heard it."

Bethany and Bre stared at one another. "Great! We're dealing with something the phone company can't explain."

Bre whispered, "You aren't kidding, are you?" Bethany shook her head no. Bre glanced around the restaurant, then back to Bethany. "Well, back to the basics."

Bethany looked at her sister. "Basics? What are the basics?"

It's something Michael always reminds me of." Bre smiled. "When things look impossible, there's a God of the impossible, and when no one knows, He knows" as she pointed upwards.

Bethany nodded. "Him and those doing it." The meal ended with both being encouraged.

The weeks passed quicker than she had expected when Bre suddenly realized Carlos' parents were due to arrive. The thought brought a smile to her face; she was anxious to meet them. She had managed to have Michael and Deborah over for dinner to meet Carlos, which went so well, it was nearly midnight when they left. Then there was a dinner for Michael and Bethany, and finally, for Carlos to meet Bethany.

It seemed like one thing after another and adding to the stress was the flashing light she had occasionally seen while reviewing her tapes. It was while speaking with Carlos about which night would be best to have his parents over, that she received the call from Randal informing her he had found her mother. For a brief moment, she didn't want to know. There was just too much going on.

The thought of facing this, on top of it all, seemed like it might put her on overload. So, she decided to set up an appointment for the following week to receive the news. Carlos' parents would be leaving, and then she could deal with it.

"I need a vacation." Bre mentally stopped to calculate how long it had been since she'd had time away to relax. "Before Mom and Dad's accident. That was over two years ago; no wonder I'm stressed."

She picked up her phone and called Bethany. "Randal called, and I've set up an appointment for Friday of next week. Are you interested in going with?" There was no hesitation coming from Bethany.

"Absolutely."

Bre smiled while considering how her life had changed. She felt like she was living someone else's life.

Carlos watched Bre's face; the stress was apparent. "Why don't we plan on eating out with my parents and coming back here for dessert?"

Bre smiled. "Why my Love? Don't you think your mother would approve of my cooking?"

Carlos drew her into his arms. Their love had erupted and consumed them. He desired to be near her, and, his thoughts were continually on protecting her. "Your cooking is wonderful, and my parents would love it, but can't you impress them with an amazing dessert as well?" You're tired - too much, love. Let's not fuss over the trivia."

Bre moved closer, and Carlo's mouth sought hers. Moments later they both pulled away shaking. "Soon Love. Let's do this right." Bre nodded and wondered what he meant by soon?

Later that evening her mind drifted to vacation again. "I wonder where she is. Would she be close by or in another state? Maybe someplace she could vacation, and with that thought, she drifted off to sleep.

Carlos texted the next day that his parents were at his home and they would see her the following evening for dinner at Montes at seven. Perhaps dessert at your place?"

Bre smiled, "Okay." For once she was glad for another to take the lead.

She spent the day arranging appointments, as she had neglected her schedule for weeks. With an interview set for Billy Martin evaluation, she finished the evening visiting an individual at home for follow up.

At the last minute, she called Bethany to see if she had eaten or was free for dinner. Half an hour later they both spotted each other coming from opposite directions, laughing they shared a hug while entering LaTeTe's, Bethany's favorite eatery. "Isn't it strange. I've never been here before." Bre's eyes surveyed the surroundings the decor presented a welcoming atmosphere with spacious seating. Once seated, she took several minutes to look over the menu, and finally decided to go with Bethany's recommendation.

"Carlos' parents are here, and we're meeting tomorrow night."

Bethany smiled. "Are you nervous?"

Bre considered the question before answering. "I'm excited, there's an expectation of something good coming."

Bethany smiled at her sister then pondered; my sister and soon my mother. She felt her life was coming full circle. "I forgot to tell you. I spoke with my parents regarding Mom."

Bre leaned forward. "Did they say anything?"

Bethany shook her head no. "Not much, but she did say that our mom appeared to be fearful."

Bre studied her sister. "Fearful, of what? Letting us go for adoption, being a parent, what?"

Bethany considered the question. "Mom said she seemed very concerned that no one would be able to trace our whereabouts."

Bre smiled. "And here twenty-nine years later, Randal Franklin's investigation has done just that." The rest of the meal was spent comparing likes and dislikes. After making plans for the following Friday, the meal ended on an up note. Laughing, they hugged and parted.

The following day Bre spent time preparing her Boston Cream dessert, running to get a facial, her nails and hair done. By the time Carlos arrived she was ready. She smoothed her dress and waited to the count of twenty to open the door. Bre was surprised at what she saw. Carlos' mother was a slim woman who appeared surprisingly young, as did his father. Inviting them in Carlos made introductions. His mother stood 5'4" with dark hair that curled softly around her face to fall neck length; dark eyes that lit up when she smiled; and a ready laugh that reminded Bre of Carlos. His father, like his son, was physically in shape, with dark hair and a ready smile. After introductions, Bre excused herself to prepare drinks and Carlos excused himself to help, slipping his hand around her waist as they left the room.

Once in the kitchen, he chuckled as he drew her to him, whispering in her ear, "You appeared very gracious."

Bre laughed. "But of course, I am." Holding her close, Bre relaxed. She physically felt her body release tension as she leaned against Carlos. Moments later they were seeking each other's lips.

Carlos looked deep into her eyes. "I love you."

Bre's breath caught. "I love you, too."

After several minutes, Carlos chuckled. "The drinks, they will be wondering." Quickly assembling the glasses on the tray, Carlos carried them in, setting them on the table before them. Talking was easy, and Bre realized she liked his parents because they were so like Carlos. An hour later they left for the restaurant where the meal passed quickly, and once again they were at her home. After serving dessert on the patio, the talk continued and, before anyone was aware midnight was approaching. As Carlos and his parents were about to leave, plans were made for the other nights together.

The week passed in a blur, and before long it was time for his parents to leave. Bre suddenly realized how much she liked them, and how much she would miss them. In many ways, they made up for the absence of her parents.

Then suddenly it was Friday. Bre picked Bethany up, and they drove to the agency saying little. After parking in the garage, they took the elevator up to the sixth floor and stepping out of the elevator, both turned to look at one another. Without saying a word, both hugged each other. Bre found herself wanting to cry and, when they pulled apart, she saw Bethany was.

Calming themselves, they walked to Randal's office and announced themselves. They were barely seated when Randal appeared to usher them into his office. Randal smiled and stated. "We found her, her address, and quite a bit of information regarding her. There were a lot of rabbit trails - almost as if to throw an individual off. "She has had several names; she's now married, so, of course, she has her husband's name."

After waiting several minutes, Bre said. "And?"

Randal smiled as if enjoying the suspense. "Your mother's name is - was Lisa McCord. After giving birth to the two of you, she vanished and resurfaced in Texas five years later to change her name to Shawn McDonald. She had this done legally, with her social security number changed as well. Again, there is nothing until five years later, and again, a name change - this time to Riley Monroe. Bre and Bethany looked at one another. Two name changes. Why?

Bethany asked, "When she changed her name the last time, was she in Texas?"

Randal shook his head "No, she had moved to Virginia."

Bre glanced at Bethany. "That's across the country. Who does that? Does she have family there?"

Randal smiled. "Good question. Her parents, your grandparents, had moved there, but she's living back in California. It doesn't appear she was in Virginia for more than a year."

Bethany spoke. "So, her name is now Riley?"

Randal shook his head no. "She changed it again five years ago, apparently just before moving to California. She was in Tulsa, apparently for a year, as there is a requirement, and she changed it to Charlie."

"Charlie?" Bre and Bethany glanced at one another. "That's a strange name to pick." Her voice trailed off. Bre looked at Bethany. "The names she picked could be a man or woman."

"Right." Randal agreed. "She's trying to keep hidden, but why? Your guess is as good as mine. There are no warrants out for any of the given names."

Bethany asked, "Do you have her address?"

Randle handed her a slip of paper. "I do. Here's the address of where she's working." He continued. "She married four years ago, and they have a small diner that serves breakfast and lunch. It does a good business."

"Thank you." Pausing Bre asked, "Have you had any connection with them?"

Randal shook his head no. "I did eat at the diner, good food, but I just had a meal. They would have suspected nothing." Bre and Bethany left deep in thought with neither speaking on their way down. Once off the elevator, they walked to their car silently.

Bre sat behind the steering wheel. "Your parents' discernment of her being fearful was on the money."

Bethany turned to look at her sister. "Yes, but why? What would be so bad you'd change your name three times and move continually?"

Bre said. "I don't know, but I'm going to find out. I'm going on vacation, and I think I know where I'm going." She glanced at the address in her hand.

Bethany looked at her. "I was considering a vacation myself. Mind if I join you?" Bre smiled as she backed out.

Chapter 5

It took a week to get everything lined up with Bethany. In the end, both were able to shuffle a few appointments. Carlos decided to take advantage of their leaving to fly to Brazil to check out operations there; which left Bre time to tie up any loose ends before going. Bre arrived early Saturday morning, and Bethany programed the address provided by her secretary. Since learning of her phone being listened in she had her secretary make the arrangements and the address given revealed a new condo on the outskirts of town.

Five hours later, Bre pulled into the outskirts of town and after checking into the condo, unpacked. After glancing at the clock, which showed twenty till two both turned to one another. The question was evident to both of them.

Bethany spoke first. "Should we?"

Bre hesitated before answering. "We can at least drive by so we will know where it's located and follow what we sense once there." The thought of seeing the one who gave birth to them, and then gave them away, settled on them like a weight.

Bethany drew in a long deep breath and turning to Bre nodded. "Let's do it!" They embraced then grabbing the keys, and headed out the door.

The drive was shorter than anticipated, and they had only driven half an hour when they approached the diner on their right. It sat off the road in an almost picturesque setting. Several trees surrounded the restaurant with a bench to the left and right of the entrance. It was a brick building that would have given the impression of being a home, if not for the sign in front indicating differently. A large parking lot was allowing ample space to park.

As they walked toward the restaurant Bre and Bethany glanced at each other and smiled, reaching for one another's hand. Bre's thoughts raced; would she be there, would she look like them, would she be glad to see them, and most important, would she want to continue? As she reached for the entrance door, she hesitated. Turning to look at

Bethany, their eyes locked. If a picture speaks a thousand words, Bethany's face could tell a story. Emotions unfiltered, etched across her face: hope, joy, fear, uncertainty. Bre understood well. They were the same emotions she was feeling. Taking a deep breath, she exhaled slowly and opened the door to walk in.

The restaurant was spacious and decorated on a grander scale than one would have expected. Light cream colors with accents of mauve and blue brightened the rooms. Booths lined the walls with tables to the center. A fireplace separated the adjacent room yet joined it at the same time. Tables set along the window facing the back revealed flower gardens and a patio where those desiring the outdoors could dine, away from the constant traffic in front of the building. It was quite lovely.

"Can I help you?" A cute blonde no more than twenty greeted them. Bre glanced at Bethany, then back to the hostess.

"Yes, a table for lunch please." The hostess smiled.

"Certainly." Taking two menus she seated them by the window, and after receiving their drink orders, left.

Bethany glanced around. "Do you think she's here?" She'd barely gotten the words out when a petite female entered through the back door. Dark hair framed her face; curling around her neck. She stood around five feet six inches, slim, and apparently in excellent condition. Her deep blue eyes surveyed the dining room. Several couples were finishing up their meals. A glance at Bre and Bethany brought her head up. A small smile came quickly to her face, but her eyes studied them carefully. Pausing at their table, she greeted them. Bre noted the lines of casual remarks to be questioning also.

Their waitress returned with their drinks, and it was at that moment they both knew they needed to make a move. The waitress left to give them more time to study the menu.

Bre turned to her mother "Does Feb. 28th, 1995, and N. H. Hospital, mean anything to you?"

Her mother's face was puzzled for just a moment; then with a sharp intake of breath, her mouth opened but no words came.

Bre held her breath. "Please let her be honest," she silently prayed.

Her mother took one step back looking intently at both of them. She gave a glance around the room, and reached for their menus. "Come with me." Bre and Bethany rose to follow her out the same door she had entered and to a patio table set among trees.

Once seated, Bethany reached for her mother's hand. "I'm sorry we didn't know how to reveal ourselves."

Their mother's words surprised them. "How did you find me?" The color that had drained from her face had returned, and her face looked flushed.

Bre spoke. "My adoptive parents were killed two years ago. It seemed like it was the right time to search for you."

Her mother repeated the question. "How did you find me?"

Bre and Bethany glanced at one another. "I retained a private investigator."

Her mother stared at her. "A private investigator - a private investigator was able to find me?" She looked shocked.

Again, Bre and Bethany exchanged glances. "Yes, they were also able to find Bethany for me." Bre smiled at Bethany.

Her mother closed her eyes for several minutes. When she opened them, her next words shocked both of them. "You don't know what you've done. Has anything unusual happened? Are you being followed?"

Bethany and Bre stared deep into each other's eyes. For a brief moment, Bre considered keeping the past few weeks to herself but decided against it. "We've both had some unusual things happen to us, as of late."

The mother was quick to ask. "As of when? "Think back - when?"

Bre wasn't sure what she had expected, but it wasn't this. Taking a deep breath, Bre said, "Since I had begun the investigation to find Bethany and you."

Her mom closed her eyes again. When she opened them, she stated, "Tell me what you know and when it began."

Bre began to tell her first of all that the investigator had discovered. Her mother shook her head as if she was still trying to believe it.

She quietly whispered. "All that I did to protect you, and here you are." Bre and Bethany looked at one another not knowing what to say. After a moment of silence, their mother said, "Tell me what has been happening that's unusual." Bethany shared about the phones and Bre told of the home invasions.

Bre watched their mothers face change from one emotion to another: fear, anger, determination, and, finally, what appeared to be a calm knowing. She turned to her daughters. "Tell me about yourselves. Are you married? Where do you live, work?" The next several hours were spent sharing about their lives.

"What are we to call you? Lisa? Charlie?"

Charlie smiled. "It must be Charlie, as that's what I'm saddled with now." A smile surfaced causing her face to brighten up. "You look like I did at your age. The hairstyle is different, of course, but the resemblance is noticeable." She glanced at Bethany and smiled at the blonde. Bethany laughed and turned to Bre who was debating on how to continue the conversation.

"The name changes. Why did you continue to change your names? Was that so we couldn't find you?" Bre searched her mother's face for the truth.

Charlie looked from one daughter to the next before she spoke. "I had hoped, with me gone; you would be safe. As you can see, I was wrong on both counts."

"Who is looking for you? From whom are you running?" Bethany had barely spoken the words when the side door to the restaurant opened.

A gentleman who may have been in his late forties, but had the look of someone much younger approached. His bright smile gradually faded as he saw the look on Charlie's face. His eyes swept over Bre and her sister. Bre had the distinct impression that an opinion had been formed, based on the similarities.

A slight smile quickly replaced the look of concern, and as he reached the table, his hand reached for his wife's shoulder. Gently rubbing it, he spoke softly, "All has been taken care of, and we are ready for tomorrow." Glancing at Bre and Bethany, he continued. "You looked as if this meeting was important and I didn't want you to be disturbed."

Charlie smiled. Her eyes lit up, as she gazed at her husband. "Daniel, I'd like you to meet…" She hesitated for just a moment before continuing, "my daughters." A slow smile spread across Daniel's face.

"I suspected as much." He reached out to take hold of both girls' hands. "The resemblance is obvious." His eyes searched Charlie's. "And…" He let the word hang in the air.

It was apparent theirs was much more than just a marriage. The two looking into each other's eyes were speaking in a language only they understood. Nothing missed, as if they knew each other's thoughts.

Daniel knew what Bre and Bethany desired to know. It would depend upon their mother, as Daniel indicated with a simple, "And…"

Charlie turned from Daniel; her eyes glanced past her daughters; it was clear she was anticipating her next move. Bre and Bethany glanced at one another. After several minutes, Charlie spoke. "Do you have plans for this evening?"

Bre spoke first "No, none."

Charlie glanced at Daniel who nodded. "You can follow me." As she rose, she stated "If you suspect you are followed, turn off in another direction and call me later." She reached into her pocket, retrieving an order form and pen, she quickly wrote her phone number. "Do you understand?" The question hung in the air.

The girls nodded and quickly gathered their purses. As they walked to the door, Bre suddenly realized there was a sense of fear that had sprung up from somewhere. Where? "Who knows?" She thought "Maybe it had been there all along and had laid dormant until this moment."

As they slid into Bre's BMW, the thought entered her mind, "My life will never be the same." Little did she know, Bethany was thinking the same thing.

"What have we gotten ourselves into?" Bethany asked as she turned to her sister.

Bre just glanced out the window. "I don't know if we just got ourselves into it. I think we've always been in it. We were just unaware." Then after a long moment of hesitation, she added, "We were unaware, and the others were as well."

Chapter 6

   Charlie slowly pulled out of the garage at the back of the restaurant. She glanced at her reflection in the mirror; her eyes looked hollow. Learning to sleep with one eye open started early, as a teen. She had no understanding of what was taking place, but the gift of discernment had been activated at ten years of age when she woke to see an apparition standing before her. From then on, she was aware of the invisible realm. It would be many years before she was aware of all that was involved in the field of the unseen watching her.

   Glancing at her daughters in the BMW that slowly backed up to follow at a safe distance Charlie thought, "My daughters." she shook her head. Who would have thought when she woke that morning that twenty-four years would resurface in the face of her daughters? "God help me! What am I to do; how do I explain?"

   Her mind flashed back all those years ago; only twenty, giving birth to twins. Unable to keep them, adoption seemed the perfect answer to her dilemma.

   Suddenly she was back in the hospital, those many years ago, remembering the long delivery that finally brought forth the two dark haired beauties. The memories resurfaced, along with sadness and grief; recalling how the nurse had asked if she wanted to see and hold them; knowing that soon she would be handing them over to two other families. She had nodded yes, remembering tears filled her eyes. "Oh, how do I make them understand?" She was given one as the nurse stood by holding the other one. Suddenly she had to be alone with them; to speak to them; to try to make them understand. It was like knowing somewhere in their spirit, in their sub-conscience, they would grasp the truth; at least that was her sensing then.

   The nurse had placed one daughter at her side, while she held the other in her arms. "I'll be outside if you need me."

   Turning, she left; leaving Lisa alone with her daughters. The years rolled back and along with them the feelings, raw and alive, surfaced. Tears slowly rolled down her cheeks, as the memories as real and living as if it had happened yesterday, played across her mind. She saw the tiny fingers; kissing each one; holding and stroking the faces. "You don't understand what I do, I do for your good. Please believe me; if I could, I would keep you." Remembering her words, "I'd die for you, but I can't have you die, too, so I have to give you to someone who can care for you. Someone who can give you what I can't." Her tears fell upon each face as she kissed and stroked them.

How did she get here? The events she now faced was not how she had planned her life. She had considered and was pursuing a degree in law; it was there in college that she first met Ben. Both in many of the same classes, it was natural for them to talk, and eventually, begin to study together. She had liked his dark looks, soft voice, and humble demeanor. It was obvious he came from a wealthy family, but you wouldn't know it by the way he acted. He was kind and generous; with a dry sense of humor that had everyone laughing when he interjected his comments; causing others to see a serious situation suddenly comical.

Ben. She had loved him and had fallen hard and fast. It seemed natural to be together. It wasn't something she had planned, and when she found out she was pregnant, she was in shock. Looking back, Charlie shook her head. "Why wouldn't I use something to prevent a pregnancy?"

The first time they were intimate was not planned. Their passion erupted until, lying beside each other, they knew there was no turning back. Still, I could have used something afterward. Charlie glanced in her rearview mirror and smiled. Her daughters were beautiful, well educated, and had chosen wise paths to pursue in professions. She was glad she had carried them and glad she had placed them in good homes with good families.

As she drove, she reflected on the day she was going to tell Ben. She was two months pregnant and, with only a few weeks left in the semester, she felt the time was right. Ben apartment was in an upscale area a few blocks away from the university. She had lived in a dorm with Sunny her roommate. Sunny was quiet and considerate; the ideal roommate, but they seldom spent time together. Once she had begun to date Ben, his friends became hers, and she rarely spent time with anyone else.

Wednesdays were their free afternoons. Remembering back, she smiled, it certainly didn't turn out as she planned. Stopping for Chinese, she had unlocked the apartment with a quick knock. "Hello, I'm here," Ben yelled hello from the bedroom and appeared in the doorway with a towel wrapped around his waist. She still remembered the leap of her heart and the smile that spread across his face. The world vanished while their focus rested on one another.

Lying in bed afterward, Ben pulled her close to him and softly whispered, "I haven't told you, but I'll be leaving when the semesters end. I'm planning on spending a few years in Europe studying."

Charlie remembered her heart had seemingly stopped or was she holding her breath? Trying to sound casual, she had replied. "Really. I wasn't aware you were interested in studying in Europe."

Ben seemed to be weighing his words. "It would help to learn the finance systems in many countries." He kissed her neck. Suddenly she had no idea of what to say or how to say it. Her silence spoke for itself, "You know I care about you," he whispered. "Perhaps you can visit." Still soft-spoken, his word cut like a knife. What did the song say? "Killing me softly with your words. Killing me softly."

She told herself to breathe. "breathe Lisa, breathe." Taking a deep breath, she pulled back to look him in the face, and forcing a slight smile said, "I'm sorry. I thought this was more than a casual romance."

Ben studied her face. "Have I lied?" Did I promise you anything?" The words, though spoken softly, penetrated like cold steel.

"No Ben." she had barely whispered, "You didn't."

Forcing a smile, she slipped out of bed. "The Chinese is probably cold." How she had made it through the evening is still a wonder to her; as were the next few weeks, but she kept up the pretense. At last, the semester ended and Ben packed for Europe. The day he left she had called to wish him well, but the phone was answered by his mother; who told her he had already left for the airport, and she would not be able to reach him at this number. She had hung up thinking, "Did I not even deserve a goodbye?"

The first signs of anger began to surface. Charlie had never met Bens family. "I guess that should have been a sign." She recalled the one time she remembered being driven to his house, he needed to pick up a computer for a friend. The circular drive made an impression, lined with trees that ended just before the front of a house that looked like a castle to her. It spread to the left and right.

She would have loved to have walked in but, Ben seemed to be in a hurry "I'll be right back" he said as he slipped out of the Jaguar. Why didn't I see all of this? The abruptness of his mother caused her to bristle. "I'm carrying your grandchild," she thought as she stared at the phone.

She remembered throwing herself on the bed and sobbing. "God, what am I to do? If I go home pregnant..." She wouldn't allow herself to think about it. She was so drowning in her emotions; she hadn't heard Sunny enter the apartment, or the soft knock on her door.

Moments later she felt the warm hand touch the top of her head. "Lisa, it's going to be okay."

Suddenly unable to carry on the charade, "You have no idea." She sobbed.

Sunny stroked her head. "You're pregnant, aren't you?"

She remembered her surprised look, as she stared at her roommate. "How did you know?'

Sunny studied her face. "I knew I was to help you. It was a logical guess." They sat and talked for hours, and as the dawn began to make an appearance, a plan became apparent.

Sunny had graduated with her nursing degree and was moving three hours away to begin her new job. Three hours wasn't far, but far enough that the likely hood of running into someone from their area wasn't a concern. She would stay at Sunny's apartment, and work until delivery. It would give her the time needed to arrange the adoption. The thought had saddened her, but once she learned she was carrying twins, she knew it was the only option. With the plan in place, she had fallen into an exhausted sleep and woke hours later; determined to carry out those plans.

It took a week to get everything arranged and to move. Charlie's mother was excited to hear she had gotten a job and would continue her schooling at night. It was the first of many lies.

As Charlie drove, she reflected on the memories of long ago - remembering the town; how lovely it was; and the hope of a new beginning. What did the novel say? "It was the best of times and the worst of times." She had been able to land a job within a week and, of all places, at a law office working for one of the attorneys. She had planned on continuing there after the adoption. The weeks continued into months. She had been in the process of meeting with prospective parents when she had learned she was carrying twins. It could have complicated the process, but they brought another family into the adoption process. The rush of the days had drifted one to another so that when she reflected upon Ben, it was to shake herself. "What was I thinking? Why didn't I see I wasn't special to him; that he never loved me?" As the anger began to surface, she told herself, "It's your own fault," but as the babies moved within her, it was only loss that she felt.

With just a month left till delivery, she had kept her focus on the adoption, and meeting several times to get to know those who would raise her daughters.

It was with this in mind that she was able to move forward and put Ben in the past. So, when the past surfaced, she was in shock. Sunny had dropped her off to grab a to-go order from their favorite Italian restaurant. Leaving the place, she looked up to see Adam, Ben's best friend. He smiled and said hello before his eyes dropped to her swollen belly. Lisa remembered her shock. She was barely able to manage, "Hi" before reaching Sunny car as quick as possible.

"Was that Adam?" Sunny asked as soon as she slid in.

The look on Lisa's face told her the answer. Lisa turned to Sunny. "Do you think they still stay in touch?"

Sunny glanced at Lisa's belly and whispered: "Let's hope not."

After being on edge for several weeks, she had just begun to feel things were okay when her world turned upside down. She'd left work and stopped by to pick up Sunny uniforms at the dry cleaners. She had approved the adoptive parents, which resulted in her signing the legal papers, giving away her little ones and although she knew deep inside this was best, the ache never left her. She had all this playing on her mind as she made her way out to her car carrying the uniforms. As she drew near the car, she lifted her head and stopped dead in her tracks. Ben stood leaning on Sunny car. Ben, the love of her life. Now the look that proceeded from him made him look like anyone but the Ben she remembered. Ben's eyebrows drew together. His piercing eyes bore into hers. "When are you due?"

Lisa's mind went into calculation mode. He must not know it could be any day. "Six weeks," she spoke the words that could be believable.

He nodded. "My parting gift?" The look on his face betrayed his feelings. Who was this man; or was he always this way, and I never saw it? Fear, raw and real, filled her heart. Ben raised an eyebrow, "If it's a boy, I will take him. You can have it if it's a girl." After hesitating, he spoke. "Unless there is a need for her."

Lisa forced herself to speak forcefully. "I'm well able to care for my child," remembering not to give away the fact that it was twins.

Ben glared at her. "You are naive, aren't you? You have no idea of my bloodlines." Then, without waiting he stepped away from the car. "I'll be back within two weeks, and we will take it from there." Then, without so much as a glance, he walked away.

Charlie watched him as he drove off, suddenly panic as real as anything she had known surface. She waited until he was out of sight before driving home.

One look at Charlie's face and Sunny she stopped setting the table. "What's wrong?" As Charlie spoke, the words tumbled out. Sunny glanced off in the distance. "He's not kidding." At her words, fear returned.

"I need to get you out of here to someplace safe." Sunny's mind was clicking a hundred miles an hour. Before long she smiled, "I know just the couple." She grabbed the phone and began to dial. Before long she began talking and walked into the bedroom for a short while. When she returned, she was smiling. "It's all set. You will love this couple, and," Sunny said, "they will love you."

Sunny motioned for her to sit down. "Dinner is ready, and you need to eat," Charlie remembered how she had looked at that moment. Sunny face showed the determination to see her settled and safe. She had been such a friend never dating during their time together, and it wasn't that she couldn't. Sunny, with her long blonde hair and blue eyes had caught the attention of many an admirer, but repeatedly stated it could wait till this episode was over. Charlie had encouraged her to date but she had just smiled.

Sunny glanced at her. "I think I'm going to take off a few days. I haven't had a day off since I've been here." She glanced at the phone again.

"I'm calling in with a family emergency", and without waiting for a comment she reached for the phone. She made the call and hung up a few minutes later to say, "I'm getting two days off.

That way we can get everything done." The evening had passed quickly; she had packed what few things she had and stated she was ready. Sunny studied her face, "I'm going to miss you, you've become family." Slowly tears began to slide down her face. They both cried. Sunny because she already sensed the loneliness, Charlie because of the uncertainty of the future. It wasn't until bedtime that Sunny brought up the topic of Ben's comment regarding his bloodlines. "I knew he was wealthy, but not in the rich and famous?"

 Charlie remembered his face; the narrowing of his eyes! A cold shiver ran through her. "Something sinister there."

Sunny nodded. "I sense it, too."

The night passed quickly, and with little delay, Sunny moved her to Gil and Ruthie's. She had liked them immediately, and any fear of intruding was washed away by their welcome. She was given the only other bedroom, with a bathroom of its own.

From there Lisa and Sunny left to get her car. She had been shopping for weeks and had settled on a gas saver, two years old. The interior and exterior were in perfect condition; the tires were like new; with low mileage. She had paid cash for the vehicle and realized, if she had not been in such a desperate situation, she would have been pleased with her purchase. Now it only served a purpose. They had taken the information and ran to Sunny insurance agency. After obtaining the insurance, they went to the Secretary of State to get the new tags.

Her back had been screaming all day, and she just wanted to sit down to rest. It was as they drove to get the car so they could put the tags on it, that she felt the first pain; and involuntarily reacted to it. Sunny glanced at her.

"Was that a contraction?" Charlie slowly nodded. They wasted no time getting the tags on, and Charlie drove back to Ruthie's with Sunny following. That even was etched forever in her mind. The hours Sunny sat with her, Ruthie and Gil both worked, so they had retired, but Sunny remained until five the next morning when she had driven her to the hospital. The day passed in a blur; the pain; the long delivery; still Sunny remained. Finally, with, the babies gone, she came into her room to rock her, as she sobbed into her chest. Four days later she was released, and Sunny, again, collected her to take her to Ruthie and Gill's; talking late into the night. Sunny had become very conscious and looked continually to make sure no one was following her. It would become a habit that she would take up.

A week with her parents and she pulled out; not knowing where she was going; only that she must go. It had been just over two weeks, and she knew Ben intended to keep his appointment with her. She was just as determined that he wouldn't.

Chapter 7

Bre and Bethany had remained silent on the drive to their mother's house; both lost in their thoughts; both were continually replaying the conversation in their minds.

Bre kept recalling her mother's face as she said, "I had hoped, if they were unable to find me, they would be unable to find you." Who were they? Her mind recalled the home invasions, and her sister's statement of her phone tapped by someone. Were they the ones her mother feared? If so, they had found them. The question now remained; was their mother known to them as well?

Following at a safe distance, Bre glanced in the rearview mirror as often as she watched her mother's car in front of her. Daniel had trailed them from behind. She was not entirely sure why, but she trusted that he had his reasons.

Suddenly, her mother pulled into a hidden drive; both sides surrounded by trees. She followed her back to a clearing, revealing a beautiful setting, and in the center, a Cape Cod home. Charlie disappeared as she drove into the garage. Daniel drove past them to the back of the house. They slowly stepped out of the car to stand and survey their surroundings. In front of the house was an English garden with a variety of flowers, beautiful to the sight and smell. A small stone path led to the front of the house with a full porch, complete with a porch swing that beckoned to them.

Charlie appeared moments later to motion them in. Stepping inside, Bre felt instantly at home. The feeling so surprised her; she glanced at Bethany to see if she had any reaction and was feeling the same.

The house was beautifully decorated in soft pastels. Light flooded in from windows and skylights, giving a bright sunny disposition. Suddenly, Bre wondered, "Do homes have personalities?" Memories of past families who had lived there, happy moments that remain in the atmosphere? If so, this house did. Charlie seemed to sense what she was feeling.

A smile caused her face to light up as she asked, "What do you think of the house?"

A strange question indeed to be asking; considering their meeting, and why they were here; but Bre smiled. "It's lovely. Thank you for inviting us into your home." Charlie asked if they would like tea. Bre glanced at Bethany, and both smiled. "Yes. We'd love some."

As Charlie left to prepare the tea, Bre walked to the mantle on the fireplace. Several pictures set on top; a family picture she could only assume was her mother with her family; a man and woman set in the center with Charlie to the left and another girl to the right; then a picture of Charlie and Daniel on their wedding day, smiling into each other's face. No other photos were seen anywhere in the room.

Charlie returned with the tea, as they sat Bre mentioned the picture on the mantle. "Yes, it is my parents, your grandparents and my sister." Both glanced at their mother, after several seconds Charlie said: "sit here." She left the room to return several minutes later, in her hand was a half a dozen pictures. One of her in a hospital bed with two small bundles one in each arm, Charlie looked worn, the long delivery apparent on her face but greater still a sadness etched deep in her eyes. Another of her holding one baby looking into its face tears visible as they flowed down her face and the third, a tender kiss on a pair of tiny hands.

From deep within Bre a sadness rose and threatened to erupt, whether the grief of the loss of her adopted parents or the awareness of the profound sacrifice of her biological mother; she was not sure, but it was there. She fought to control the tears that threatened to flow.

Two more pictures were made available. In one a man was smiling; having dark hair and eyes; his smile toying with the one photographing his image. His good looks were visible, but there was something else; a knowing; almost a smirk playing at his mouth.

The next was of the same man and their mother, a younger version but just as pretty. The man held her as she smiled at the camera; his arms around her from behind; holding her close with his face next to hers, as he, too, laughed.

"Our father?" Bethany asked the question. Charlie nodded. Bre spoke. "Tell us about him." The next several hours passed with no interruptions. Occasionally a question would be asked by Bre or her sister. In the end, Bre glanced at her watch to see five hours had passed.

"You never mentioned his last name," Bre glanced at her mother. She spoke it softly, looking to see if either recognized it.

Bre was the first to react. "Do you mean..." and she spelled out the name letter by letter. Charlie nodded. Bethany and Bre exchanged looks. "Well, it's known for money." Bethany glanced at Charlie, but Bre was looking out the window, her mind searching, where had she heard that name? " Aren't they involved with international affairs? It seems I heard it mentioned involving the government."

Charlie glanced at her watch. "I've never Facebooked, and the little I've heard on the news was unrevealing."

Charlie Rose. "I'm going to whip up something. You must be hungry."

Bre stood "No, we've taken enough of your time." At the look on Charlie's face, she quickly responded. "We're here for a week, there will be time to visit."

Charlie asked, "Will you stop by tomorrow at the restaurant?"

Bethany glanced at Bre. "Not tomorrow, but Wednesday. It will give all of us time to sort everything out." Charlie nodded then stood as if not knowing what to do. Bre reached out first, placing her arms around her mother; holding her. She sensed a genuine need to protect her.

Charlie had shared some of the times of the years following her giving birth; hard times; fearful times; and lonely times. She determined her future wouldn't be the same. Bethany was next, and as she held Charlie close, Bre watched her mother's expression. A tenderness covered her, causing her entire body to relax. Bethany released her with a gentle kiss on the face. There was no way to describe the look of love and joy on her face. Waving goodbye, they made their way to the car. Once inside, both sat silent for a few minutes.

Then Bethany broke the ice. "I'm starving." From somewhere deep inside of Bre, she started to laugh. The release of tension caused Bethany to join her, and for several minutes they sat laughing until they cried.

"Let's get some food," Bre said as she started the car.

They found a Mexican restaurant and made their way inside. After ordering, Bre asked, "What did you think when you learned who our father was?"

Bethany stared at the chips and salsa. Slowly she lifted her head to stare at Bre. "After what I learned, not much."

Bre nodded. "There is something there." She slowly repeated his words. "You are naïve aren't you. You have no idea of my family's bloodline." She glanced at Bethany, who lifted her eyebrows.

Suddenly, Bethany reached for her phone and began to search the web. In just a matter of minutes, she had what she was looking for, and turned her phone for Bre to see.

There he was smiling broadly to the cameras and with him a dark-haired beauty at his side. "Is that his wife? She's young enough to be his daughter." Reading the caption underneath revealed it was indeed his wife of five years. His former wife had drowned years earlier. They had one son. A shiver ran down Bre as she handed the phone back. They ate, both lost in thought, then they drove back to the condo to undress, and fall into bed mentally and physically exhausted.

Chapter 8

Ben glanced at his phone. Shelton wasn't to call unless there was a problem. His eyes narrowed. "Excuse me, please. I must take this call." Those at the dinner party smiled and nodded, while Cilia lifted an eyebrow; her way of asking if everything was okay. Ben raised his eyebrow for her to take note he wasn't sure. Cilia was sharp to the ways of business, especially his businesses and she wanted nothing going wrong.

His mind drifted quickly to Elizabeth, a total opposite to his present wife. Elizabeth was blonde and fair; educated in the best of schools. She had a grace that others noticed and welcomed, where Cilia was a dark-haired beauty that drew attention where ever she was. Those were not the only differences. Elizabeth, raised in Europe, had tired of her family's money. She remembered the nannies who replaced her parents' presence, and she vowed it wouldn't be that way in her home. Although her family was involved in governmental affairs, there was no desire to follow suit. She was also quite naïve, which proved to be of great value to Ben. She neither cared nor wanted to be a part of his world of finance. A home and a family that she could care for and she was happy. Cilia, on the other hand, had also been raised in Europe, but had determined to climb as high as she could go; as fast as she could get there; and would do whatever she needed to accomplish that.

It was just a matter of time before she and Ben would meet with his many business connections in Europe. Ben remembered the first time he met Cilia. She had walked in the room, and all heads turned. As introductions took place, she stared into his eyes; her lips played with a smile, and he knew he had to have her at any cost. That night he had managed to arrange for a quick meeting to consolidate future meetings. She never left his apartment, and from that moment on, she never left his mind. Elizabeth had been a good wife, a good mother, but she would fight a divorce, and Ben knew it. The only solution was to take matters into his own hands, which he did.

Matthew, their son, was in his twenties and dating seriously. He would miss his mother as they were very close but would survive. Ben wasn't sure he would without Cilia, and so he had planned the weekend at their lake house. A glass of wine before Elizabeth took a nap allowed him to place a sedative strong enough to drug a horse in her drink. Dropping her off in the middle of the lake could have gotten messy, but he had enough connections there was no investigation. Looking back, he wondered how he had managed. An autopsy would have revealed the truth but Matthew was devastated, and Ben wanted to get rid of the evidence quickly. After a proper viewing and cremation; he gave her ashes to Matthew to do with as he wanted. Hiding his relationship with Cilia for six months while playing the sad widower was not easy, but once he and Cilia were married, he was able to breathe easier.

Shelton's voice sounded hushed as if he was unable to talk freely. "The price has gone up.”

Ben glanced out over the lake. “How much?"

"A hundred thousand," Shelton answered.

Ben paused. “Have you looked over the merchandise?”

Shelton was quick to answer. “Yeah, top quality.”

Ben spoke. "Make sure the transporting is secure. I don't want any foul-ups."

“I’ll see to it.” The phone went dead. Ben ran his hand through his hair smiling slightly, and walked back in to join his party.

Charlie glanced at her calendar the week was nearly gone. "Then what?" she wondered. Would visiting with her daughters again be an option, or would they disappear? Glancing at her watch, she realized they would be arriving soon. This week had been a gift she never thought she would see and now that she had, she couldn't lose it. She was lost in thought when the doorbell rang.

Daniel answered, and soon Bethany and Bre stood before her. As they sat talking, Daniel excused himself to prepare dinner.

Charlie drank in her daughters' appearances. They had changed during the week. It was hard to describe, but their facial expressions revealed it all. When Charlie mentioned it, Bre and Bethany glanced at one another. It seemed to be so. Something had changed. Bre had lost the deep sadness in her eyes that had remained since her adopted parents' death, and Bethany had a softness that was expressed, not only by her ready smile but a joy that was apparent in her face.

Bre was the first to answer, "We see it in you as well."

Charlie smiled, "My greatest dream has come true." Charlie's smile lit up her face and, just as quickly, faded as she whispered, "And my greatest fear."

"What are you afraid of, Mom? What is it that has kept you running all these years?" As Bre spoke the word "Mom," Charlie's head jerked up. Mom was not a name she was expecting but, once spoken, something deep inside of Charlie reached out to grab it; and with it; a determination to never let it go. Whatever came down the road, they would face it together. Never again was she willing to let them go.

Bre watched her mother's face; the different emotions were apparent on her face; then, suddenly, the determination. Charlie drew in a deep breath. Her mind drifted back over all those years long ago, and she began.

"You know how they tell when you are in a dysfunctional family? No one knows it. It seems normal because it is their normal." The girls both nodded. Charlie glanced out her patio window. "I wasn't aware of anything as being abnormal until later. Oh, I sensed something, but," she hesitated, "it's not that my parents were abnormal. They were good parents and treated me well. There was no abuse, emotionally or physically but there was always something; a something I didn't notice or was actively aware of until I was pregnant with you two. Then I began to see in the spirit realm. Bre glanced at her sister to see her face turn ashen.

Bethany asked, "What do you mean, see in the spirit realm?"

Charlie said, "What you see here. She motioned with her hand around her to the patio furniture. "All that we see, there is more. There is an invisible world that lives and moves around us."

Bre asked, "Why did you become aware of it when you were carrying us?"

That's a good question." Charlie said and glanced out the window. "I'm not sure I have the answer, but after I'd seen your father, I knew he was serious. There was just a fear that you needed to be hidden and protected. I've questioned my decision at times, but most of the time, I knew it was best."

"Has seeing in the spirit realm continued?" Bethany asked.

Charlie nodded and turned to Bethany. "You see, too. I could tell by your face. When did it begin?"

Bethany took a deep breath. "When I was small, I woke to see something standing by me and staring down. I screamed and woke my parents. There have been other times. What does it all mean?"

Charlie glanced at her daughters "I'm not sure other than gifting; that offers some form of protection. I've found it's better to see than not. Do you dream?" She glanced at Bethany, but it was Bre who raised her hand.

"I've had dreams from the time I was a little girl; dreams that came to pass; it used to scare my mother."

Charlie nodded. "I can understand why but there's not too many who do." They all sat silent for a few minutes.

Suddenly Bethany said, "You know we could be quite a team, with both of us seeing and you dreaming. We could advertise" if you need help call the dream team." She smiled, but there was a look that crossed Charlie's face.

"That's not as strange as it sounds." There have been many times when I would have loved to have known someone with both of your giftings."

Daniel entered at that moment to say dinner was ready. Over dinner, talk drifted to the future and how they would meet.

Bre was once again sensing that same ache she had known since her adoptive parents perished in the car accident. Her thoughts drifted to moving. Could she? More important, should she? It would be difficult. She then thought of Carlos and Michael. It would take a lot of careful thought, as there were others to consider. She slowly shook her head. Unbeknownst to her, Bethany was thinking the same thing. She glanced at her mother. Daniel was the protector she needed, she could rest easy knowing that.

The day ended too quickly, and soon all were standing at the door. Plans had been made for monthly meetings. Saying goodbye was difficult. Bre spoke first on the way back to the condo, "Wouldn't it be interesting to meet our father without him being aware we were his daughters."

Bethany glanced at her sister. "Our father! Are you serious?

Bre kept her eyes on the road. "Wouldn't you like to know what he is like?" Without waiting for an answer, she continued, "Remember, we have a half-brother." Bethany was silent so long that Bre glanced at her.

 Bethany stared out her side window and slowly said, "I'm just trying to adjust to meeting my mother."

 Bre reached for her hand. "I know. Just something to consider for the future." Bethany smiled and nodded.

Once home, things seemed different. No longer did Bre's focus remain on what was, but what is, and what could be! The thoughts of meeting her father continued to brew. "I wonder what he would be like and would he want to know them"? Remembering her mother's warning, she hesitated. What if he didn't know she was his daughter; she could somehow meet, and form some relationship with him. Her mind continued until, finally, she called Michael. She hadn't seen or talked with him since she had been back and had only seen Bethany once. Carlos was due back in a few days, and she decided to move; at least get as much detail as her brother might be able to obtain. She called asking if they could meet for lunch.

"It's about time. I've been waiting." Michael laughed, then pausing, "I wasn't sure how the meeting with your mother went and didn't want to intrude." Bre smiled. Her brother had always been loving and considerate where she was concerned.

"It was wonderful! When can we meet?"

Michael hesitated, then answered, "Let's meet today. I have a free lunch schedule."

Soon she was sitting across the table from Michael, filling him in on the week away. Michael listened intently saying little. It wasn't until she mentioned her father's name that he sat up straighter.

"Are you kidding me?"

Bre studied her brother's face. "Have you heard the name before?"

Michael nodded. "There's not many who wouldn't recognize the name that was aware of the world affairs and government."

After a moment's hesitation, Bre said, "Michael, I was wondering if you could search me. I know Mom wouldn't want it, but I'd still like to find out about him." Michael sat back, surprised not regarding the request, but by his sister's comment. "Mom, wouldn't want me to." The sudden realization that his sister was indeed past the mourning of their parents was a good sign, although it stung a bit hearing her call another Mom.

"I can try. I can't promise anything." Michael smiled.

Bre squeezed his hand. "Thank you! I love you!" The lunch ended, and Bre drove off feeling much had been accomplished in the last two weeks. She wasn't the same person. As she glanced in her rearview mirror, a habit she had developed after meeting her biological mother, she wondered how much her future would impact her. She was soon to find out.

Chapter 9

   Carlos arrival was a much-needed diversion. It seemed as if he'd been gone a month, or was it that so much had happened in the short time he was away? When he arrived at her house, his smile and the throaty laugh was all she needed. She sank into his arms, feeling the tension released from her body. After kissing her face, neck, and lips, his eyes searched her face. She had asked that they not contact each other on her vacation while visiting her mother. Though they had talked briefly over the last several days before leaving; it was apparent he was worried about her.

   Bre rewarded him with a bright smile, and while sipping on tea, she shared all that had taken place over the past weeks.

   Carlos listened intently then smiled. "I'm glad your reunion with your mother was satisfactory. Sometimes one doesn't know." Bre knew what he meant.

   After a moment of hesitation, she shared what she knew about her father and her desire to at least meet him.

   "Are you sure that's wise? Especially if your mother has real concerns." Bre studied Carlos' face she wanted him to relax and trust her instincts.

   "I've asked Michael to see what he could discover."

   Bre was ready to change the subject. "What about you and your parents? How are they?" They spent the evening talking and, at the last minute, grabbed a bite at a local diner. Carlos left late that evening, lingering at the door. Bre realized how much she loved him. What would have happened if he hadn't entered her life? Looking back, she realized it was as if he began a domino effect with everything shifting in her life, all at once.

   The following day she heard from Michael. "Why don't you come over tomorrow night for dinner?" Deborah is visiting her mom's, and she'll be out of town for a few days."

   Bre considered the offer. "Would you rather go out to eat?"

Michael laughed. "No! I'm still able to grill a mean steak." After making the arrangements with Michael, she got busy with her clients. It took the rest of the day to contact those in her case file and to arrange their appointments.

Bre's focus throughout the following day was her meeting with her brother. She knew Michael well enough to know he wouldn't have contacted her unless he had something to share.

She arrived early bringing a dessert, and to help prepare the meal. Michael took his time broaching the subject of her father.

Finally, over dessert and coffee, he looked at his sister. "Your biological father is under suspicion by the authorities.

Bre realized she had been holding her breath. "For what?"

Michael picked up his coffee. "Trafficking."

Bre stared at her brother. "Michael, are you sure? I mean where did you get your information?"

Michael hesitated. " I have friends in high places, and there are several areas of investigation concerning him."

Bre sat silent for several minutes. "What kind of drugs is he in?" Michael's facial expression made it clear he was debating on how much he should say.

Finally, he drew a long breath in and said, "It's not drugs – it's girls. He's into sex trafficking." For a second it didn't register. Trafficking-that was selling girls for sex. Why would her dad be selling girls for sex? From somewhere deep within her, a wave of anger rose screaming to the surface. Selling girls! Her mind raced to the teenage girls she had dealt with in the court system.

Without thinking she was up, pacing back and forth., "The sorry, no good..." Suddenly overcome by emotions, she began crying. Tears rolled down her face.

Michael was up in a second. He pulled her to him. "I'm sorry! I debated if I should tell you." Bre buried her face into her brother's shoulders.

"Mom was right, she was right. "The tears continued and after many minutes she pulled away. Michael handed her his handkerchief and walked her to the patio. There under the stars, she wondered aloud. "How could someone from such an influential family end up in the sex trade?"

Michael studied his sister. "His family fortune is questionable. There have been links with organizations that run decades back, highly secretive and worldwide."

Bre starred at him. "What will it take for him to be taken down?"

Michael stared at her "Bre, it's enough to know that he's is observed. It's just a matter of time, and he is going down."

Bre was back up and pacing. "You mentioned his family. Mom said they were very wealthy, but she was never invited into their home. One time she was with Ben when he stopped quickly to get something, she said it looked like a castle."

Michael observed his sister. He had seldom seen her like this. Remembering the accident that claimed the lives of their parents, she was like a one-person army, determined to know the why's. Nothing stopped her until she had the truth on the table; no rock was left unturned. "Bre, you have to stop; we don't have all the facts."

"You may never have the facts. Justice can take time, and many can be bought off." Bre was angry; it showed on her face; and for the first time, Michael was concerned.

"Bre these people are dangerous. You need to calm down and consider what you are saying!"

Bre pointed at her brother. "Don't you get tired of the injustice that is in this country? Young girls! Michael, Young Girls." She was yelling.

Michael grabbed Bre and held her. "Stop," He whispered, stop." Almost as one who calms a child, he whispered over and over, until at last with a deep sigh, she nodded. Michael led her back to the patio seat. "I will be pushing the investigation; trust me."

Bre nodded, but her mind was racing. She was already making plans to contact Bethany and her mother. What would they say? After another hour, Bre helped Michael straighten up and after reassuring him she was well, she left.

Glancing at the time, she called Bethany. "I know it's late, but I need to talk with you. When can we meet?"

Bethany glanced at the clock. "Will tomorrow work?"

Bre realized she'd awakened her sister and whispered, "Yes. Tomorrow lunch at Monte's" and hung up.

That night Bre tossed and turned. She woke up tired and angry, not the good combination. Her meeting with her sister couldn't arrive soon enough, in the meantime she called her mom. She had bought a new phone under another name, but still, she knew better than to talk on the phone. A simple meeting was planned for an earlier date, two weeks earlier."

Her mom knew immediately; she was speaking of the following weekend. "That sounds wonderful" Bre hung up thinking, "You may reconsider, once you've heard what I have to tell you."

Bethany arrived a few minutes early, and Bre was glad. She'd been sitting there for twenty minutes already.

Bethany took one look at her face. "What's up?" She knew her sister well enough to know she was concerned about something. Over lunch, the story unfolded. Bethany's mouth dropped open, and she sat there dumbfounded for several minutes, in the same position.

"I know! Can you believe it?" Bre was fuming again. "Michael said he would push the investigation, but you and I both know it can take a long time. In the meantime, what is happening to these young girls?"

Bethany shook her head as if to clear it. "We have to think on this. You're reacting, and that's never a good thing."

Bre looked at her sister. She was right, of course, but how could you not? Still watching Bethany's demeanor, she calmed herself. I mean what did she think she was going to do; march into her father's organization; and demand he turn those girls lose? She was only one person, and how did she think she could arrange that? But once the thought came, every avenue came to her mind and slowly, calmly, she began discussing the options with Bethany.

Bethany's eyes widened. "Look, I know you're upset, but you need to slow down! You don't know what you're dealing with!"

Without thinking, Bre answered. "You sound like Michael."

Bethany lifted an eyebrow. "There's a reason. Your brother is at the top of his profession and over the rest in the area."

Bre sat back. She wasn't one to quit and to do nothing. Doing nothing was making her feel like a quitter. "I've called Mom, we're meeting next weekend. Did you want to come?" Bethany nodded her yes, and said, " let's change the subject and put our heads together next week at Mom's." Suddenly Bre was ready to let it drop, at least verbally, but her mind was still running with one option after another.

Chapter 10

The week passed too slowly. Bre did all she could to keep Carlos from knowing the direction her mind was going, but he was too discerning. Finally, after dinner one evening, she shared she would be going away for the weekend to visit her mom.

Carlos studied her face and in his direct way asked, "Bre, what's going on? You've been distracted for a week?"

Bre drew in a deep breath with all intention of passing it off as nothing, but when she saw the look of love on his face, she knew she couldn't. "Carlos, my father is selling young girls! Women! He's into sex trafficking."

Carlos straightened up, looking at the love of his life. Without thinking, he pulled her to him. "I'm sorry; I know what this must be doing to you." Bre looked into his eyes. The compassion and hurt that he knew she felt were evident on his face. From somewhere deep within her, something began to break, it shook her to the core. She couldn't even speak. For several minutes he held her as she silently cried.

When she was finally able to speak, she said, "It's not for my dad; it's the girls". Carols nodded and continued to hold her. Emotions spent, she got up to wash her face. Moments later she returned and was surprised by Carlos's question.

"What do you intend to do?"

Bre explained. "I have Michael investigating. He said he's running down every piece of evidence he had, but you know how long that can take. He even mentioned that his family's fortune joins with other organizations that date back generations old and could be quite dark."

Carlos nodded and then asked, "Is that the reason for your visit with your mother?" Bre nodded yes, he then asked, "Don't you feel it's time for me to meet her?"

The question took her by surprise then a slow smile spread across her face. "Would you like that?"

Carlos studied Bre. "Are there any reason between us that I should not meet her?" Bre shook her head no. Then Carlos said, "I think I should meet the mother of the woman I love."

Bre smiled. "I think you're right. We're leaving Friday afternoon. I'll let her know you're coming."

Later in bed, Bre's mind ran a dozen directions; what would it take to set her father up? How could he be caught? At long last, she fell asleep and woke the next morning with a new determination to do what was necessary to see her father pay for his crimes.

Friday arrived with Bre, Bethany, and Carlos driving to her mother's. It was dusk before they arrived and Daniel motioned them to park in the back. There they found a separate garage for three vehicles. The door was open, and they drove in. As they gathered their overnight bags, Charlie stepped out the patio door.

"Welcome. What a nice surprise to see you early." Bre laughed and hugged her, and then turning to Carlos, she introduced him to her mother. Charlie's expression remained the same, but her eyes searched Carlos' face. Bre recognized she was testing his spirit, and when a smile lit up her face, Bre guessed he had passed the test. Bethany joined with a hug and Daniel motioned them in.

The smell of dinner filled the air, and Bre suddenly realized she was hungry. After some small talk, all gathered around the dinner table to enjoy the buffet Daniel had prepared. Bre kept silent about her dad until the meal was over, and they had retired to the patio. Bre waited to bring up the topic until she felt the timing was right, which didn't come until Daniel excused himself saying he needed to retire. He would be opening the restaurant early the next day.

After good nights, Bre turned to her mother. "I've learned of where Ben is but most importantly, I've learned of what he is doing." Charlie lifted her eyebrows and waited. Bre glanced at Bethany and Carlos then back to her mom. "I had Michael run a check on him. He's under investigation for trafficking girls. He's into the sex trade business."

Charlie was silent for several minutes as she glanced beyond them; her mind recalling the last time she had seen Ben. "He's been educated in the international banking business. He would know the ropes and would have many connections." Charlie glanced at her daughters. "How long?" she asked.

Bre shook her head. "Who knows." Michael is trying to run down every trail he can."

Charlie glanced at Bre. "You mentioned, 'under investigation.' So, he is now under the eye of the law?"

Again, Bre shook her head. "So, I'm told."

"For sex trade?" Charlie asked.

Bre turned to Bethany. "Well, I assumed it was that because Michael mentioned there was a suspicion, he was involved in it so..." She left the sentence half finished.

Her mother turned to her. "What are your plans?" Carlos had asked the same question, only differently. "What do you intend to do?"

Bre answered, "Whatever I can, but as Michael and Bethany have repeated to me, I can't just run off without a plan."

Charlie nodded. "We need to sleep on it and see what we come up with tomorrow."

Bre suddenly realized she was tired so she stood asking, "where would you want us to sleep?" Charlie escorted them to a large bedroom with two double beds. Bethany's and her overnight bags sat deposited on the beds, "the bathroom is right next door." Bre thanked her and glanced at Carlos as he followed her mother down the hall to a bedroom of his own. His over the shoulder look brought a soft laugh to her, as she glanced at her sister. Before the hour was over, both were sound asleep.

Bre woke the next morning, showered, and dressed, to find Carlos in deep conversation with Charlie and Daniel. As she entered, they stopped.

Bre hesitated. "Did I interrupt something?"

Carlos said, "I would be the perfect candidate to be able to infiltrate your father's business, with my nationality he would be less suspecting."

Bre's mouth dropped open. "What are you talking about?" She glanced at her mother, who again shrugged.

"You acted as if you were serious to do what you could to expose him and take him out."

Bre looked from one to the other and finally settling on Carlos, she asked, "What are you talking about?"

Carlos glanced at Charlie and Daniel then back to Bre. "There is always a demand for such a business. The very fact that we employ many men for the business might cause less suspicion. I first thought to bring them in for a party but decided it wouldn't be permanent enough. They would want individuals who would invest in an ongoing exchange. Only then could we nail something on them."

Bre listened, "How could you even make the connection without it being obvious?"

Carlos answered, "Hopefully, that would be where your brother would come in. He may be able to find out his connections and contacts." Bre's mind was running, and it was obvious. She began to walk back and forth, as she pondered on what he said. "It could be dangerous. It's not worth it to me."

Carlos looked at Bre. "You know you will never be able to let this go."

Bre stopped. "What if I was somehow able to get captured?"

Carlos was now up. "No! I don't know how they work all that out, but I'm not willing to let you put yourself in that position."

Charlie spoke up. "Your brother, Michael, will be the key in all this; how much he knows to be true; and his ability to get those undercover to work with you." The truth of what she stated became evident, both to Carlos and Bre, she nodded. Bethany chose that moment to walk in, with brunch served.

Later that evening Carlos, Bre, and Bethany began the trip back. Bre smiled; the trip had been successful. Her birth mother had met the man her daughter loved and who loved her. She was content to be a part of her life, and although the topic of Ben's activities was a concern to her, she left feeling pleased.

Bre arrived home and immediately called Michael, to ask if lunch Monday would be available for him. After confirming its time and place, she unpacked. The rest of the weekend couldn't pass quick enough and, finally, she was seated across from Michael in the restaurant. "What have you learned about Ben?"

Michael hesitated. "Not enough. We know he is smuggling women and young girls into the country. It's perfect. This nation has no record of their citizenship. If something happens, there is no one to call and report them missing."

Bre nodded. "How are you aware of this?" Her brother was silent for several minutes until Bre spoke. "Michael, I recognize the position you are in and what could happen if this got out, I wouldn't ask if it wasn't crucial."

Michael nodded "I know, still I'm only able to reveal so much. I can say that one of our men was caught red-handed and spilled the beans on the operation. I think he thought he'd make a lot more money doing the same and hoped to branch off. It was a lucky break for us. Although I'm not directly involved, I have access to the information, just because of my position, and what comes through this area."

 Bre asked, "How connected is Ben? Does he keep out of the mix?"

Michael waited until they had given their order to the waitress and then answered, "I think that has been his running plan, but since this new wife, he's more involved. That's where you get caught."

Bre sat in deep thought, then asked, "Do you have any informers involved?"

Michael shook his head. "That would be our ideal procedure, but other than Nicks confession, we haven't been lucky enough."

Bre glanced out the window. Turning back to him she asked, "Would someone like Carlos work?"

Michael's head jerked up. "What are you talking about?" Bre replayed Carlos' discussion with Charlie and her." Michael shook his head. "He doesn't know what he's getting into and just because of his nationality doesn't mean he'd be beyond suspicion."

Bre then asked, "What if it was something, he was asking for himself or his employees? A party or something," Bre finished lamely.

Michael considered the question, "It would take some real brainstorming."

Bre studied her brother. "Do you think something like that could work?"

After several minutes had passed, Michael said, "There are a few ways that we could go at it." Bre held her breath. "If he were to go in setting up an escort service, he would need women and young girls. But that also means he would have to have a place to keep them. That could get expensive. I don't know how they work it, or how he could get hired working for him. Either way, you take a chance of him finding out, and I don't believe he is beyond murder. The death of his first wife has raised some eyebrows." Michael continued, "I guess you have to ask yourself, how important is it to you?"

Bre's mind went back over her past cases. There had been several that had torn at her heart all sex trafficking cases, one girl was barely thirteen. She was fortunate to make it out with her life. It takes years for them to trust and to enter into society again but was it important enough to risk anything happening to Carlos? The thought was enough for her to want to withdraw, but it had been his idea. She wasn't sure if he would want to.

"How long would it take to get him nailed?" Bre waited for her brother to answer.

"There is no guarantee of time. It might be two months to two years. That's the chance you take."

Bre asked, "Would you talk to Carlos? If it's dangerous, I'm not sure I'm for it." Then, as if speaking to herself, "I've just found him I don't want to lose him." Michael suggested meeting Friday, as it would give him time to see what else would surface.

Chapter 11

Stella sat listening to the report given. Nickolas made sure the report was complete and every area covered. Stella didn't like surprises and had ways of making you wish you'd been more thorough. He waited for her response. She looked out the window; glancing across the lawn, and her pen gently tapping against her lips.

She was a good-looking woman for her age, of course having money for whatever you needed made a difference. She had to be in her early seventies; still slim, and though her face wasn't faultless she was still attractive. Light brown hair that she kept highlighted and blue eyes, you would never have thought by looking at her that she was as cold as ice and would bury you in a heartbeat if you got in her way. Nickolas wondered where her mind was and what her plan was for her son's illegitimate twins.

Stella turned to Nickolas. "So, all attempts to enter Breanna's home have been stopped?"

Nickolas nodded. "Her brother has kept it under lock and key with armed security 24/7.

Stella's eyes narrowed. "But you have the phones tapped, both her and her sister's?" Nickolas nodded affirmatively. "What about her sister's townhouse? Are you able to enter there?" Stella asked.

Nickolas nodded, then spoke when he saw the look on Stella's face. "We have and can, but it's like she went through the place with a fine-tooth comb. Since her meeting with her sister, and comparing notes she's shut every door."

Stella thought of Ben. Since he'd married his new wife, Cilia, her son was no longer the careful member of the family he had once been. She shook her head. Not that she particularly cared for Elizabeth, his first wife. She was such a worm which was of course, the reason he'd married her. Pretty and pleasant enough, but oh my, so naïve. Stella pursed her lips not so with Cilia. No, she knew what she wanted and intended on having it; which was fine as long as she didn't get in her way. She was young and would want an heir. Matthew would sooner or later follow in his father's footsteps, or would he?

Matthew was like his mother. She knew he had no idea of what Ben did and wondered why it never entered his mind. Like his mother, he too would rather dwell on the pleasant. No. She wasn't sure that Matthew would follow at all, which meant Ben would need an heir to continue the bloodlines.

Her thoughts drifted to Breanna and Bethany, her son's stupid mistake. Not only one but twins that could contend with her grandson and future heirs' inheritance, and then the legacy. It was fortunate that Ben had confided Lisa's pregnancy to her. She immediately had sought some of their members to stage the transfer, but before they could, Lisa had slipped out and away. It was only through bribery that they were able to discover she'd had twin girls, but where and to whom they were give, they were clueless. That is until Randal Franklin had slipped. One slip that's all it takes, and one slip it was. It was a casual mention that Bre, heir to millions was looking for her biological birth mother. The slip was made over dinner and drinks to one of their members. Not realizing the importance of what was said it was weeks before it reached Stella. The age of Bre would have been the same and the fact that she knew she had a twin sister was too much of a coincidence. Stella moved quickly. When the monthly members met, Ben was informed. Stella could have informed him privately, but he needed a wakeup call. Since Cilia, he was no longer family focused, and he'd forgotten the oaths and vows that allowed them to live the life they did. Maybe the thought of losing it would wake him up.

Stella refocused and glared at Nickolas. "Are they aware of who their father is?"

"We are unaware of that. We have only recently considered tapping Randal's phone," Nickolas replied.

Stella stood. "Why only recently?"

Nickolas was quick to respond. "We had their phones tapped. If they called Randal, we would have them recorded anyway."

Stella leaned across the table. "Some respond through email. Is that being looked into?"

Nickolas nodded. "We have their business email. We are aware that Breanna has contacted her sister and met. We're on it."

Stella dismissed him with a nod towards the door. "Then finish it!" Nickolas nodded and arose to leave. Stella called to him as he reached the door, "Leave no stone unturned." Nickolas turned to give a salute and left.

Bre called Michael. "Is Friday still good, and would I be able to come?"

Michael, who knew his sister well enough to know she would ask for it, smiled. "Yes, I'll see you at one."

Manuel had arrived yesterday. As the agent in the investigation of receiving and transferring the women, he was able to fill Michael in on the activity there.

Suspicion of some of the police paid off was troubling. Having the police and other involved paid off was dangerous. Michael had wrestled with that all day. He still wasn't sure of the best way to go.

Bre and Carlos arrived on time. Greeting Michael, they were surprised to find Manuel there. An hour into the conversation, the topic of the police being bought off came up. It caused both of them to sit back in their seats. Bre's eyes met her brother's and Michael lifted his eyebrows with a nod towards Carlos.

"I'm not sure that's the way you want to go. It could get dangerous."

Carlos rubbed his chin and glanced at Manuel. "You seriously believe there are members of the police force that are being paid off?"

Manuel said, "There's no other answer for the near misses. There have been several times when we were minutes away from intercepting the incoming shipment of women, and no one was there. Somehow they had been informed!"

Carlos, deep in thought, asked, "So what do you suggest?" He turned to Manuel.

Manuel was debating as well. "There can be no connection with the police. It will have to be us alone."

Carlos nodded. "But have you been able to connect with Bre's father?"

Manuel said, "That, too, will have to kept from the police, I'm not willing to take a chance on anyone."

 Michael asked if there was some way to get close to him.

"He seems to be pretty closed off, although we are aware that he likes to entertain the big guys when they're in the area. The main thing is to be located in the area, and get set up so you have a home base. They're only hours from here."

Carlos and Bre eyed one another. They knew the time of decision was here. Either they drop the matter and go on with their lives, or they activate a plan. The primary need was to have a strategy and work it well.

Michael turned to Manuel. "You're going to be here a few days, correct?" Manuel nodded. Michael continued, "Okay, let's get back together on Monday and spend the weekend focusing on 'the plan.'"

It was clear Michael and Manuel were going to continue the discussion, so Bre and Carlos slipped out. A glance at the clock revealed they'd sat in Michael's office three hours.

Carlos asked Bre if she was ready to eat, or would she rather wait a few hours.

"Let's unwire first. Why don't we head back home and meet in a couple of hours at my house?"

"Sounds good." There was too much circling in her mind, weighing everything. The seriousness of the situation weighed heavily on her conscience. Was Carlos doing this for her? If something happened to him, she wasn't sure she could handle that.

At home, she rested. Lying down allowed the body to relax but did nothing for her mind. After a while, she gave up and began to prepare dinner. When Carlos arrived, she had everything ready. Though they tried, it was hard to talk of anything but the discussion earlier. Relaxing after dinner, Bre turned to Carlos. "Why do you want to do this? Is it just because of me?"

Carlos was silent for several minutes, and when he began to speak, he pulled Bre close to him. "My family had good friends for many generations. Because of the family's business, we have earned respect from even the authorities. We employ many families. One family that has been with us for many years had a daughter who turned up missing. We did all we knew to do to find out what had happened. We finally recruited a private investigator. They found her on the bathroom floor of a home whose primary use was that of a brothel; her innocence taken; her soul stained, and her spirit troubled; not to mention her mind. We paid for her recovery, one year in America where she stayed, to heal and be made whole. Today, five years later she is pursuing law in her efforts to sow good from what was bad."

Carlos shook his head, "when I visited her the first time I thought "How can money mean so much that individuals could do this to another person, especially this innocent young girl?"

Bre nodded. "Some of my cases were also girls involved in sex trade. People can't imagine the damage it does." Carlos nodded. They talked deep into the night.

"If the government thought that this involved terrorists, we would have their cooperation." Carlos turned to Bre. "Is that not true?"

Bre considered the question, her mind racing. "Absolutely, but I would have no idea how we could work that into this or even imply it." The evening ended with nothing on paper or in the mind that was worked out.

Saturday, Bre was wakened by Michael knocking on her door. She answered, sleepy-eyed. "It's nine o'clock! Since when did my sister sleep in until nine?"

Bre smiled and motioned him in. "I didn't get to bed till three."

Bre saw the look on Michael's face and explained. Michael said "Manuel feels we can bypass the police and go directly to the feds to have something installed in his house and on his phones."

Bre stared at her brother. "If it was that easy, why hasn't it been done before?"

Michael smiled. "Ben has his home and yard carefully patrolled, but they are installing a new pool. Manuel received the news this morning from his partner. If we can replace one of the laborers with one of ours, we may be able to pull this off."

Bre was quiet. "It sounds a lot easier than I think it's going to be, and I still don't know how they can get to his cell?"

Michael smiled. "They have their ways."

Studying Michaels face Bre was able to relax. If Carlos didn't have to be involved in this, she would be happier. With her mind at rest she suggested he call Carlos with the news. This weekend suddenly looked a lot better.

As Michael made the call Bre suggested he come for breakfast. After a quick shower, she returned smiling. Michael had started the coffee, and she began to mix up the pancake batter. They worked like a pair used to being in the kitchen together. Bre laughed, remembering their childhood days, "It's your turn to set the table."

Michael laughed. "This does bring back memories, doesn't it?"

Bre smiled and nodded. "Good memories."

As Michael studied his sister, he became aware that she had changed over the last year. Carlos had been perfect for her, and it was obvious he loved her. He expected marriage to be forthcoming and would be glad to welcome him into the family. His thoughts were interrupted by the knock on the door.

Bre opened the door with a smile. Carlos smiled and nodded to Michael as he leaned close for a kiss from Bre. He motioned to the table, "What can I help you with?"

 Bre smiled. "we have it all under control. I'm pouring pancakes, and about to fix the eggs. How do you like yours?"

The breakfast set the stage for a relaxed conversation regarding Ben and the new information. Carlos listened intently. " It would be nice if it were that easy."

He glanced at Bre who replied. "That was my exact statement."

Michael glanced out at the patio area. "Sometimes things fall into your lap; you stop a truck, and they are carrying an arsenal; you get a call, and it's a tip that breaks up a drug ring. You never know." He glanced at Carlos and Bre. "This may just be our lucky day," he said as he lifted his glass of orange juice to theirs.

Chapter 12

Monday, Carlos and Bre rode together to Michael's office. Manuel was there with a tall gentleman. Upon entering they all stood. Michael made the introductions. Quinn Nelson had been with the FBI for twenty years, working his way up the ladder while serving in several divisions. Sex trade had become an interest of his when a close friend's daughter was taken while on a cruise. For several years she was missing, until one of her friends Mark, spotted her while on vacation in the islands. She had glanced at him, and her eyes motioned to her friend to say nothing. She had continued walking with the two men who were with her one on each side. Mark decided he was not going to ignore what he saw. Instead, he paused to look at souvenirs; then followed them at a safe distance.

After seeing the building, they had entered Mark quickly contacted Quinn who moved quickly. Within hours he and several agents had landed and entered the building where she was. Because of the surprise, there had been little resistance. Notifying the police came after placing her on the plane. The men were apprehended and put in jail; but they knew to keep their mouths shut or they and their families would suffer for it.

As Quinn related the story you could see an anger surface. "No one should be able to rule over another's life, and I'll spend the rest of my life to ensure that."

Bre looked at Carlos; his face revealed the determination felt. "How difficult will this be?"

Quinn glanced at Manuel and answered, "Hopefully not difficult at all."

Over lunch, information revealed the plan. Quinn and Manuel would be expected Thursday of that week, to begin the work. The ground was ready, and they would spend the next two days working with a company that would be providing the material. Together they would work with their work crews and would have one of the foremen with them, during the installation. They would keep Michael informed. The lunch ended on a high but serious note.

Tuesday and Wednesday Bre found it challenging to work. She canceled her appointments, and with Bethany drove to see her mom. Charlie was surprised as the girls walked in the restaurant unannounced. As was her custom Charlie studied their faces. Recognizing this they both smiled brightly and a moment later they were sitting at the outside patio as Bre filled their mother in on all the information they had.

Charlie listened intently. After Bre had finished she glanced around the patio area and spoke softly. "I hope it goes as smoothly as they hope. When are they beginning to lay the pool?"

Bre answered, "Thursday."

Charlie nodded " we will be praying that all goes well." Over lunch, Daniel joined them suggesting they spend the night at the house instead of the hotel.

Bethany glanced at Bre who nodded. "If that's not putting you out?"

Charlie's smile widened, "Never! And if you like call Carlos and invite him."

Bre smiled. "He's catching up on work. He has been so involved with this; he hasn't focused as much as he probably should on his business."

The day passed beautifully with Charlie sending them on into the house. Once there, they unpacked their few belongings and wondered aloud if they should prepare dinner. Deciding against it, they chose instead to make reservations at a restaurant in the area. A quick call and the time set for seven.

The evening passed too quickly Charlie and Daniel enjoyed a meal made by someone other than them. While eating they laughed about the many disasters of their recipes of the past. Laughing helped Bre and kept her from focusing on what was about to take place. Still as she laid her head on the pillow that night, she knew she needed to return the next day and slept restlessly.

Once back, she busied herself writing up recommendations for the court, and as the evening neared called Carlos to ask if he wanted to grab a bite out. He had just returned home and suggested they call Michael and Deborah to see if they would want to join them.

Bre made the call and Michael answered, after listening to Bre he passed.

"Sorry, Deborah had dinner started. Let me check with her to see if there's enough."

Bre interrupted. "No thanks. It was just a thought" she laughed, then added "Call me if you hear anything. Remember, it's this number now."

The evening passed too slowly. Bres mind ran continually. "Just get this over." Carlos talked calmly but after he left, she took a PM pill, and fell into a hard sleep; only to wake up tired wishing she had left the sleeping pill alone.

Thursday dragged and went into Friday. Bre thought she'd scream if they didn't call but at last Michael called. "A bug is in the kitchen and what looked like a master bedroom."

Bre said, "What if they are whispering?"

Michael answered, "Bre, these are very good. They will pick up a whisper fifty feet away, to get two placed was a miracle."

Quinn had waited until the second day to ask if he could use their bathroom. Cilia had brought drinks out the day before, and he hoped she would again. When she showed up with a tray, he was ready and quickly asked if it would be too much of an inconvenience to use their bathroom. Ben was gone, it was one of those rare chances."

The relief Bre felt was unbelievable. She felt her body physically relax. "So how long before we know anything?"

Michael answered, "He didn't know." Then he mentioned that Quinn had stated there was a house for sale directly across from Ben's home. He said it would be an excellent lookout but was sure it was up for a pretty penny."

After hanging up, Bre couldn't get the idea of the house for sale off her mind. She called Carlos to ask if she could stop down.

He laughed. "Of course," though he may have wondered why Bre would want to come to his place. The truth was she wasn't so sure her house was safe and not watched. It was a fact that stayed on her mind.

She quickly drove to Carlos' to relate to him what Michael had said. Carlos, like her gravitated to the house across the street that was for sale. "That would be a great place to survey all that goes on. If we had that Quinn could stay there, and it would make things extremely easy."

Bre suddenly said, "I think we should look at it."

Carlos looked at Bre for a long moment. "You know it will be expensive?"

Bre nodded. "We need to get the address and agent selling it and use your name."

Carlos smiled. "Are we to be Mr. and Mrs.?" He pulled her close. "Would that be of interest to you?" His smile was wicked and played upon his lips. She realized how much she loved him. He took her breath away even in the midst of all this, and she found herself smiling when she thought of him.

"Would you want that to be of interest to me?" She looked into his eyes.

"Bre, I love you. You know that don't you? Nothing would make me happier than to make you my wife. I want to ask your brother if you agree. I beg your forgiveness, this was not the way I had intended to propose."

Bre laughed. "I love you too, and would be honored to be your wife. I'm not sure how we could pull it off quickly though. It can take up to a year to plan and reserve a wedding," Bre said as she glanced out the window, "unless Michael could arrange something at the country club. April isn't the month for weddings so we may be able to pull it off. If we make a list for the invitations; I could have Bethany help me, and we could have it out in a week. I'm not sure about a dress though."

Carlos smiled. "Anything you wear will be perfect."

"Okay then, I'll call Michael and ask when I can see him." Bre smiled and said, "Why don't we stop over now?"

Carlos looked at her with a smile. "It may interrupt his evening."

Bre smiled. "Well, let's just see!" Picking up her phone she called Michael. "Are you busy tonight?"

Michael answered, "Actually I'm at loose ends. Deborah is out of town for a convention."

Bre grabbed the moment. "How about Carlos and I grab something to eat at your favorite Chinese place and bring it over?"

Michael laughed. "A woman after my own heart."

An hour later, Carlos and Bre walked into a set table and a hungry brother. Laughing they heaped their plates and talked for several hours. Then over coffee and cake Carlos turned to Michael.

"Michael, I have something to ask you," Michael turned, and suddenly a grin began to play on his lips.

"Go right ahead."

Carlo's cleared his throat. "I never had the opportunity to meet your parents. I know they were wonderful people, because of you and Bre. If they were here, I would be asking them, but they are not; so, I would consider it a great honor to marry your sister. She expressed her desire to marry me also." At this, he picked up Bre's hand and kissed it. "I would appreciate and honor your approval." Then hesitating, he stated "If you would feel you could do that?"

Michael stood with open arms and embraced Carlos. "Welcome to our family." Bre began to cry as Michael pulled her to him and kissed her face.

"Now, what can I do? When is your date?"

Bre glanced at Carlos. "Well, we were hoping you might be able to arrange something at the country club in about six weeks?"

Michael never batted an eye. "I'll do all that I can to arrange that but you will be a very busy girl for the next few weeks."

Bre then shared their plans to buy the house across from Ben's.

Michael whistled. "Have you thought that through?"

Bre and Carlos looked at one another smiled, and nodded. "We won't be living there just visiting occasionally but it will be perfect for Quinn and whoever would need to stay there."

Michael stated "Visit then, but carefully consider if that is the route you're to go."

Bre nodded. "I've got to call Bethany to let her know." Grabbing her phone, she walked into the foyer and called.

Bethany answered with "Hello, Sister."

Bre asked, "How did you know it was me?"

Bethany laughed. "you called on my new phone."

Bre remembered that she was one of the few programmed in. "Oh, that's right. Guess what you're going to be busy doing with me this next week?"

Laughing Bethany said, "Fill me in or it could take all night?"

Bre smiled. "Hold your breath, you're going to be helping me fill out my wedding invitations."

A squeal answered Bre. "And it's about time! When is the date?"

Bre laughed. "In six weeks from Saturday; so, we have a lot to do. Lunch tomorrow?"

After hanging up, she joined her brother and Carlos who were in an in-depth discussion regarding Quinn and the situation developing. Bre listened until Michael glanced at his watch.

"It's getting late and I have an early, early appointment tomorrow." Bre stood hugging her brother, and watched as again, Michael hugged Carlos congratulating him.

The evening ended with Carlos escorting her into her house. "Tomorrow we must look for your rings."

Bre looked deep into his eyes which appeared to be dancing. "I'd love that. I'm meeting Bethany for lunch. Do you want to join us or meet afterward?"

Carlo's kissed her on her nose. "I suspect you two will enjoy lunch alone tomorrow. I can pick you up if you'll call when done." The night ended with Bre smiling, as she dozed off.

Lunch was wonderful as they laughed and talked, each adding to the conversation until they knew where they would go to look at dresses. Bre knew her seamstress could design something very close to anything she chose and have it ready to wear in plenty of time. Next, came the design for the invitations as they sat scribbling at the table.

"I'll ask Carlos the given names of his parents." Suddenly Bre stopped. Looking at Bethany she asked, "Is Mom going to be hurt by me naming my parents that raised me?"

Bethany looked at her "Bre, Mom went through a lot to keep you hidden. I don't think she'd have it any other way, but you can talk with her."

Bre nodded. "Okay you're right, and I wouldn't want to hurt Michael." Bethany ran the design for the invitations over that afternoon with a guarantee that they would be finished in two days as the advertised they could. That night she and Carlos would get a list from his parents regarding extended family and friends, and she would contact Michael for a list from him. "I'm inviting Mom and Daniel."

Bethany smiled. "Of course you are; I wouldn't have it any other way." Smiling Bethany winked.

The week flew by but Bre calculated every day out; placing each assignment in a category and successfully marking it off. The dress was the most difficult as she struggled between three. Finally, Bethany suggested that the fuller one wasn't as attractive as the other two, so that was out. She then settled on one that showed off her figure but flowed down beautifully.

 After being told it would be impossible to have it back for at least three months Bethany obediently snapped enough pictures that she was able to drop them off at Adeline's who said, "Of course I can." "Oh, and change it only slightly so it's my original." Bre beamed.

The week ended with the invitations out; the dress ordered, a date set at the Country Club, and a meeting with the chef to decide what they would dine on. They even arranged for the cake ordered in four different tiers; each layer a different flavor, and the perfect ring set on her finger. Bre laughed out loud. She realized she had never been so happy.

She and Carlos, along with Bethany had driven to visit their mom and Daniel. After sharing her news, she handed her their invitation, explaining why she had her adopted parents listed as her parents.

Charlie smiled and answered, "But of course, there should be none other." Bre looked at her mom and realized she meant what she said. "They loved you; provided for you, and raised you. They are to be honored."

 "But you will come, will you not?"

 Bre watched Charlie's face as it lit up. "But of course! I'm your mother."

Chapter 13

Bre handed her ticket to the airline stewardess; Carlos followed. After finding their seats, they buckled up, waiting for the plane to take off. They could have driven but Bre wanted to get there quick. The agent was already contacted and they were scheduled to view the house in a few hours. A car was scheduled to be picked up at the rental center.

Once up in the air, Bre glanced at her phone, for once it was blank. It had been a busy few weeks, and Bre didn't want to get so caught up with activities that she forgot what all was taking place in a home across from the one she would soon be looking at.

Squeezing Carlos' hand, she smiled while closing her eyes. The next thing she knew they were landing.

"Wow, that was quick."

She glanced at Carlos who kissed her nose. "You needed the nap."

After collecting their car, they punched in the address and were soon on their way. The drive was quick, within thirty minutes they were pulling into the gated community. The agent waited for them and punched in the code as they followed. After several curves they soon pulled into a circular drive. As Bre stepped out of the car, she glanced across the street. Ben had secluded his house with a high brick fence. You could see the top of the house with the second and third floor, but little else. Hearing her name called, Bre glanced back to the house they were visiting. It was a beautiful tan build, scaling three floors, with a double door beckoning your welcome. Entering the house, she was surprised at the size of the foyer. Unlike most homes which placed the stairs immediately to the right or left, the stairs stood a good distance ahead. Bre walked through the whole house and realized she really did like the design. The rooms were large with plenty of closet space. Six bedrooms and baths made it easy to have your entire family with plenty of room for everyone, or as Bre thought the FBI.

The back was beautifully landscaped with a security fence surrounding it. A large pool and patio invited everyone to relax and enjoy themselves. A small building by the pool made for a changing room and a bathroom, along with a small kitchen for snacks and refreshments. Another decorative building set at the back of the fence, housed everything needed for the yard.

The agent stated, " Many living here have someone cut and mow their yards, as most in this community were professionals with busy lives."

Bre nodded. When the viewing was done Carlos asked the price and, upon learning the owners were moving out of the country asked if the agent thought he would drop the price considerably?

The agent remained neutral. If they had a figure in mind, she would submit it. Bre and Carlos walked thru the house again. While Carlos was speaking to the agent in another room, Bre walked to the bedroom facing Ben's house. You could clearly see over the fence, and into the yard, and she believed if one had binoculars you could see into the bedroom. As they joined her, she motioned for Carlos to look out the window. "The view is beautiful."

He looked then turned to the agent and gave a sum they were willing to give. "Let us know the answer." He then gave her his card. As they drove out, Bre glanced at her dad's house. He certainly had secluded himself... but not completely.

Upon arriving home, Michael had contacted her. "Quinn contacted me. Seems Ben and Cilia will be leaving for Europe for a few weeks." Bre waited to see if more was coming before she finally answered.

"I believe he travels there often as his wife is from there." "Yes, but he will be gone several weeks."

Again, Bre said, "Okay?"

Michael answered, "Well, let's just say there has been a lot of excitement at the Bureau."

Bre stated, "I've seen his house; it is very secluded; with a high brick fence. It would be very difficult to get in."

Michael chuckled. "Sometimes those are the best, as the seclusion helps those who get in."

Bre took a deep breath. "Well they better know what they are doing." She then told him of the offer they had made on the house across the street and how the upper bedrooms were perfect for viewing directly into his yard and upper rooms.

Michael whistled. "That's a lot of money." Bre shrugged while gesturing with her hands. "I don't think we would lose any money if we turned right around and sold it."

Michael hesitated then softly spoke, "No, unless people would rather not be around where someone lived that was into sex trafficking."

Bre suddenly understood what he was saying. "I'll just have to take the chance."

Michael continued, "I'll keep you up on what I hear." He then hung up.

The agent called the following day and Carlos contacted Bre to let her know, after a little bargaining, the owner consented. They would meet the following Monday to sign papers. Now that it was settled. Bre found her stomach doing flip-flops not really understanding why, she called her mom. Knowing Charlie was not one to carry on much of a conversation on the phone, she decided to drive down, and took Carlos with her. Upon arriving, she pulled behind the house as she was instructed before.

Charlie walked out to greet them. "This is a surprise." Charlie's smile welcomed them.

"I just needed to talk." Bre's voice shook and she mentally scolded herself. Charlie missed nothing and took Bre into her arms holding her for several minutes.

Over dinner Bre and Carlos shared about the house; what Michael had just said, and her concerns regarding the safety of everyone. "I just don't want to go through all this and wish I hadn't in the end."

Charlie eyed her daughter. "Sometimes one doesn't know until afterwards. If we knew, there would never be any mistakes or the results thereof."

Daniel remarked he felt buying the house was a good idea, "It's a perfect hideout and lookout station."

Bre nodded. "It really is." then went into describing the house. "I just have an uneasy feeling for some reason."

Charlie glanced at Daniel then said, "I follow those feelings. You may want to follow it down to what exactly you are feeling uncomfortable about."

Bre glanced at Carlos. "I will," she promised.

The visit was needed and she left feeling better. I mean what could happen after all? The week flew by and before realizing it, it was time for her and Carlos to sign on the house. Smiling Bre realized this was their first purchase. Both agreed to pay half, though Carlos had fussed about Bre putting any cash in. The purchase was in both their names and again Bre felt an uneasiness. When Carlos and Bre spoke at last about it she felt she didn't want to be around her biological father. She didn't want to meet or know him. The purchase was strictly to take him down, nothing more. As soon as he was caught she would sell. Carlos said he understood and was in agreement. Still, the uneasiness remained.

After the papers were signed, they flew out for a few days staying at a hotel, in separate rooms. For several days they visited furniture stores purchasing what was available to be delivered at the house. As the furniture began to arrive, and the house filled up the spirit of the house changed. "This is lovely," Bre smiled as she walked from room to room. After grabbing a dinner out, they returned. It had been a busy few days. Not only was furniture bought but linens for the bedroom and kitchen supplies.

Returning home from dinner, Bre fought sleepiness. Carlos woke her with a kiss. "Time to turn in, Love. You are safe, I will sleep right across the hall."

Bre laughed and after a shower, fell into bed sleeping late the next morning. She woke to the smell of coffee and bacon. As she stepped into the kitchen, she was surprised to see Quinn and Manuel.

Carlos smiled, "I connected with them last night and asked them to join us for breakfast. I wasn't sure if you were ready for them to move in."

Bre's face lit up. "Actually, anytime you're ready we are. We have extra keys made so we can give one to each of you. Will others be joining you?"

Quinn answered, "There will be others coming in and out occasionally, so as not to draw attention but we are the main inhabitants."

Several days had passed when Quinn asked if he could fill them in. "We have great reception and were able to hear clearly conversations between Ben and Cilia. The trip to Europe was to 'strengthen their relationship with the family' though I didn't sense it was relatives, if that makes any sense."

Carlos asked, "Could it be Mafia based?"

"That's a possibility, but there's something not quite normal there. You have to hear the conversation to understand what I mean."

Bre and Carlos glanced at one another. "Have you managed to get into the house?" Carlos asked.

"No," Manuel answered. "They have someone who does lawn work. We have something that when the gate opens, we are able to access the code. We are waiting till then." Ben and Cilia have only been gone two days so we are waiting patiently."

Bre looked from Manuel to Quinn. "You have something that downloads another's code?" Manuel said nothing, just nodded. Bre got up to begin to clean up. "Wow! Well you're welcome anytime. We are flying back tomorrow, so you can grab your stuff and move in."

Manuel and Quinn stood thanked them for breakfast, and stated they would return in a few hours with their belongings. Bre showed them the bedroom she had given them that looked directly into Ben's yard.

"Mine is on the same side down the hall."

After they left Carlos pulled Bre to him. "Are you feeling better about this place?"

"I'm not as uncomfortable but there is just this little something..." Bre relaxed in Carlos arms. Soon the kiss became passionate. Breathing hard, Carlos pulled back.

A smile played at his mouth. "Soon, Love. Very soon." Both pulled away and began to clean up. Later when Quinn and Manuel returned, Carlos prepared steaks for dinner.

The evening passed quickly. Quinn and Manuel wasted no time in setting up cameras along with equipment, the likes of which, neither Bre or Carlos had seen before. Deciding to leave the investigation to the FBI, the focus was instead on packing for the early morning flight.

Back home Bre stopped by Michael's office with pictures of the house, the bedrooms facing Ben's house, along with some of the equipment being used. Michael looked from one to another until he got to the one of the equipment.

He whistled. "They are leaving no chance to failure." Bre said nothing. She wouldn't understand anyway. It was enough to know her brother did and was impressed.

The next several days passed with Bre and Bethany receiving and posting acceptances to her wedding. Then there was the first fitting of the dress. She stood with her mouth open.

Bethany jumped up and down. "It's really lovely." Bre and Bethany snapped pictures to send to Charlie. The weeks were flying by when Michael called,

"The men have gained access to the house much is under lock and key. Fortunately, Quinn is able to master that also. There is a list long enough to choke a horse of previous shipments they have taken pictures of and have taken a couple of pages."

Bre's heart stood still. Finally, able to breath, she whispered, "Why only a few pages?"

"They have been obtained illegally. They had to leave the rest there and use these to obtain a warrant." Michael answered, "They see the officials early tomorrow. We'll know quickly. This may be over sooner than we think."

Bre said, "What good is evidence? If they could catch him red handed, it would be better."

Michael chuckled. "My little sister that is the plan. This will grant the investigation to run full speed ahead and give them the legal authority to rock and roll."

Bre answered, "Just so they don't mess anything up. No stone unturned."

Michael answered, "That's the plan."

A quick call to Carlos brought him to her home. As they discussed the conversation Bre had with Michael, he smiled.

"Wouldn't it be nice if we could get this wrapped up before the wedding?"

Bre smiled. "Well, it would be a great wedding present but let's not get our hopes up."

Several days passed before Bre heard from Michael again. He asked if she and Carlos could stop by his office that day.

Without hesitating, she had answered, "Absolutely!" then added, "I don't know for sure about Carlos. I'm not sure of his schedule, but I'll check with him. If he's unable, I can." Then hesitating, she asked, "Is it good news?"

Michael answered quickly. "It's good indeed."

Breathing easier she replied. "I'll see you around three." A quick call confirmed Carlos could attend. They arrived anxious to know what Michael would say. He wasted no time.

"It seems Ben and Cilia were making arrangements for a shipment of girls from Europe - you know, some like the accent. They arrived in yesterday and received the call to confirm that fourteen would be arriving this Friday. Believe it or not they are flying in and he will collect them Friday night. They fly in after midnight."

Carlos leaned forward. "How will he collect them?" Michael said, "We're not sure. That's why we tail them; never letting them out of our sight."

Bre answered. "Please don't let them blow this." Suddenly she turned to Carlos. "Let's fly down. We can be at the house."

Michael answered quickly. "Bre, it's best if you stay home. The men need to be focused and not distracted, and they may be if you're there."

Bre glanced at Carlos who shrugged his shoulders. Bre looked at her brother. "If we stay out of their way, and we will why couldn't we go? We may catch something they won't."

Michael smiled. "I doubt that, at least call Quinn and ask."

Bre nodded and stood to leave. "Thank you for keeping us up on the investigation. It's important to me to know."

Michael smiled. "I know it is. It's okay, I want this as badly as you." A quick hug and they left.

As they walked to the car, Bre asked Carlos, "Do you think I should call Quinn?"

Carlos was silent for several minutes, then answered, "I believe Quinn will be honest with you, and you'll know if you should or shouldn't.

Bre wasted no time as they slid into the car. She was speaking to Quinn, direct and to the point. She asked if it would be ok for them to fly down and be there during the bust.

Quinn wasted no time telling her it was her house, but he felt it would be better if she remained away from the house. "We're not sure what all is going down, and I'd rest better if you were out of the picture."

Bre hung up the phone, turned to Carlos, and said, "He said, 'It's your house, but it may be best to stay away.'" Carlos looked at Bre. "And?" Bre raised her eyebrow. "Well, as he said, "It is our house."

Chapter 14

Bre tossed and turned all night, finally rising before the sun. She weighed all the possibilities. Ben was picking up the girls. They weren't being delivered to his house, unless after being collected they would come to his house. She couldn't believe he would actually bring them to his house. What could happen? As she tossed the possibilities around, she kept coming back to, "Why not."

She'd love to be there when it all came down. She waited till eight to call Carlos, rehearsed all she had wrestled through, and finished with "Why not."

Carlos remained quiet on the phone. Finally speaking, he said, "Bre, if you go, I'll go too. I wouldn't want you there alone, but Quinn may be the wiser here."

Now it was Bre's turn to remain silent. She finally said, "I just don't see why we couldn't. I'd like to go."

Carlos answered, "Very well. Set it up."

By mid-morning everything was settled. Bre could tell Quinn was not liking It, and said he'd given her fair warning. But in the end, stated, "It's your house."

Bre and Carlos lifted off at seven and landed not long afterwards. Collecting their car, they pulled into their drive, not long afterwards. Bre motioned Carlos into the garage. Once inside they were greeted by two rather distant FBI agents. Bre apologized and promised to stay out of their way, quickly disappearing into their bedrooms as if to prove their point.

Carlos unpacked and knocked softly on Quinn's door. Walking into a dark room, he was motioned to a chair. Trying to explain Bre's need to be here didn't go over any better than when Bre spoke.

Quinn was direct and to the point. "In these situations, there is no sure-fire solution. Anything can go wrong, and anyone can get hurt."

Carlos quietly said he understood and they would stay out of sight. Then he asked how things were proceeding and got a "none of your business" look.

 "Tomorrow you need to get what you will need for the entire day and stay to the back of the house. We will be moving into action tomorrow night around ten I would assume, but that is always debatable."

Carlos simply nodded his agreement then said, "If there is anything I can do, just ask." This sentence just hung in the air.

The look Quinn gave him said a million words. "You've done enough." Without him uttering a single word, Carlos quietly rose and escorted himself out.

The evening passed soon enough; a hot shower, a bowl of cereal, and Carlos smiled at Bre as they parted ways at her door. "Tomorrow Quinn suggested you move to the south side bedroom."

Bre's head lifted. "Why? I can't see from the south side."

Carlos tilted his head back. "Bre." That single word spoke volumes.

"Okay! I'll move as soon as I get up tomorrow."

Carlos smiled. "Thank you. Now get a good night's sleep, Love. I'm sensing you'll be glad you did tomorrow."

It didn't take long, just a few trips to the window. Bre had brought along good high-powered binoculars and found out just how good they were, as they caused Ben's house to look as if it was inches away. However, there was little to see. The window coverings were in place, and there appeared to be no movement that she could detect. Falling into bed she was out in minutes, and slept until late the next morning.

In the morning, she quickly dressed and began to gather what she wanted with her in the new bedroom she would be moving into. Before long, she was moved in completely. She quickly made up the bed, then descended down the steps to see what was available for breakfast. The coffee sat on the table and Bre helped herself to a cup. Carlos smiled, winked and motioned to the oven. Bre opened it to see Spinach Quiche in a long 11x17 inch pan. Part of it was missing but half still waited for whoever would. Smiling, she grabbed a plate and began to dish out a sizable portion. "Where is Manuel?"

Quinn motioned upstairs. "I'll send him down. I'm finished here. We'll be eating, one at a time." He glanced at Carlos. "Thank you. That was delicious." Carlos smiled and Quinn quickly left the room.

Bre turned to Carlos. "You fixed that?" He laughed out loud. Bre smiled. "I love your laugh."

With eyes that twinkled, he winked "I love you." Within a short time, Manuel joined them. Helping himself, he ate quickly and said little. Bre and Carlos exchanged looks. Carlos cleared his throat, "I hope we're not putting you out?"

Manuel looked at Carlos first then Bre. "It's your house. Just stay out of the way." With that he grabbed another coffee thanked them for the food, and left.

Bre bristled, "It is our house you know. I mean we didn't have to allow them to stay." Carlos laughed again. Bre just sat back and smiled. "Okay, let's do this!" Together they cleaned the room and gathered enough food to feed themselves and the others, and silently walked to their rooms. Fortunately, Bre brought some files to work on and Carlos finished some billing. A mid-afternoon nap, and Bre woke to see the clock pointing to eight o clock. She sat straight up, quickly moving to the door. She cautiously walked to her old room and moved to the window. Ben's house was lit up like a Christmas tree. What was going on?

She slipped out and went to Carlos' room. He sat on the bed eating his dinner. "Hi Love, you were sleeping so soundly I didn't have the heart to wake you."

Bre began quickly telling him of Ben's house. Carlos followed her silently across and down the hall. Sure enough, the house was lit up and as they watched a long van pulled up to the gate. Bre grabbed the binoculars to look closer. The driver pushed the button and moments later the gate opened allowing him to drive in. Bre looked as far as she could but the brick hedge blocked the view.

Bre's mind went to food. "Have Quinn and Manuel had anything to eat?"

Carlos nodded yes. "I took them something an hour ago."

"Good." Slowly they walked back to Carlos' room. Bre glanced at Carlos' plate. He moved swiftly to arrange her a plate piled high with sliced ham, cheese, and crusty bread. As she reached for it she suddenly knew Quinn and Manuel had somehow managed to see what happened when the van pulled in. How she didn't know, but she knew that they had managed to place a camera somewhere, and they saw what took place when the van pulled in. She turned quickly to the door.

"Where are you going? Aren't you hungry?" Carlos stood.

Bre turned to him. "They saw what happened when the van pulled in."

Carlos looked at her questioning, "How do you know?"

Bre shrugged her shoulder. "I don't know, I just know." She reached for the door. Carlos quickly grabbed her hand.

"Bre, now is the time not to interrupt." He spoke with such force that Bre stopped. Silently she sat down on the bed. Carlos handed her the plate of food and she quietly ate.

After fifteen minutes or so, they heard movement in the hallway. Carlos reached for the door. Stepping out he asked if everything was alright.

"I'm leaving Manuel here. I'm following. They're on the move."

Carlos said, "Don't you have help? You can't go alone."

Quinn was moving quickly down the hall, and Carlos almost ran to catch him. Quinn turned. "Get back! I have back up." In minutes he was gone. As he turned back, he saw Bre slip into her old bedroom. He quickly followed.

"He has back up, he said."

Bre nodded, "He'd better have." She watched as the van pulled out and started down the street. Moments later a truck pulled up and Quinn jumped in. Quickly it pulled away.

Bre turned to Carlos. "Is Manuel still here?" Carlos motioned to the other bedroom. Without waiting, Bre entered. The room was black and Bre and Carlos stood for a few minutes for their eyes to adjust to the darkness. The light from the street lights filtered in. Slowly she made her way to Manuel. "How did you see over the hedge? How did you know what was in the van?"

Manuel turned to look at her. "It's a hidden camera. We have several around the house, and a few in the house."

Bre looked at him in shock then turned to Carlos. "I told you I knew."

"What was in the van?"

Manuel said, "That is private information."

Bre continued, "I thought they were flying in after midnight?"

Manuel glanced at her. "Who said they weren't?"

"Well," Bre begun "Who was in the van?"

Manuel looked at her and answered, "I didn't say anyone was in the van." Bre turned to Carlos who just smiled.

She asked Manuel "Is it alright if we wait in here?" Manuel turned back to the window. "It's your house."

Several hours passed. Bre very awake from the nap she sat quietly glancing at Carlos occasionally. No one said a word. Leaving only to use the bathroom she returned to see Manuel turning on camera's in different parts of the house; the one stationed in the kitchen showed into part of the living room, focusing on the door entrance. The second one in the master bedroom, revealing the large room and into the hallway. Nothing was seen though the house was lit; you could see no one, and no movement. Bre sat until she could sit no longer. She had just begun to rise when the van made its entrance. Quickly she sat hardly able to breath, the gate opened apparently from a remote control within the van.

They watched as it pulled in. Within seconds, Bre watched as several men quickly crawled underneath any security device and crossed into the yard. She glanced at Carlos who reached for her hand gently squeezing it. Silently they watched as Ben, Cilia, and several young girls descended from the van. Entering into the house from the front door, the cameras from the kitchen caught them as they entered. The four girls looked to be in their early teens. Cilia motioned for them to walk down the hallway. The master bedroom camera picked them up as they entered the master bedroom. Ben entered minutes later and handed them something to take. When one refused, Cilia quickly raised what looked to be a whip of some kind.

"My God!" Bre whispered. Ben laughed. Within minutes the girls quieted down.

Bre watched in horror as she saw several men enter the house. Older men, wearing three or four thousand-dollar suits. Ben had the girls leave with the men who took them to different bedrooms. Bre stood. "Where are you going?" "Do something."

"Shut up and sit down." Manuel spoke quietly - yet strongly. "Keep one there," he repeated to himself over and over until, at last his request was granted. The last man began to undress the young girl, as Cilia and Ben taped, videoed, and took pictures. The men had barely finished the act, when the doors broke down, as Quinn and several agents entered with guns pointed and yelling,

"Hands up! You're under arrest for sex trafficking."

Manuel jumped up at the same time grabbing his radio. He rattled off a code yelling, "Now!" Enter now!"

Suddenly Bre watched as one car after another entered with men surrounding the house. Dogs were released and stood at attention ready to respond to any command. Bre's hand was over her mouth, tears rolling down her face. Carlos seeing her reaction grabbed her close to him and held her as she silently sobbed.

It was hours for everything to turn quiet. Ben, Cilia and the older men were led away in hand cuffs. The young girls were escorted away with women officers to gather information, and following the procedures needed to prove the acts that had taken place. Bre considered offering her services then decided against it, as she worked and was licensed in another state. Glancing at the clock, she decided to wait until morning before she called Michael.

When Quinn returned hours later she asked only one question. "Was everything done legally? Was every area covered and did you have everything in order?"

 Quinn smiled. "Yes, Ma'am! Yes, Ma'am! Yes, Ma'am!"

Bre smiled. "You're always welcome here."

Quinn smiled and stated, "I'm turning in for the night."

Sleep was fleeting. Dreams surfaced. She was running, several girls ran with her, and as she glanced back, she saw Ben's angry face. She'd awaken and fall back to sleep, only to awaken from another dream.

She woke exhausted and rose to call Michael who told her he'd already been informed. "It looks solid, Bre. The warrants were already issued. The Feds had everything lined up.

"The girls, what about them?"

"They will be asked to give testimony against them. It will be placed on video. You know the routine." Michael answered. She did know the routine which was why she wanted to make sure all the I's were dotted and all T's crossed.

 Michael sat for a minute before answering, "Depends on the judge. Bre, you know the routine." He was right - she did.

Chapter 15

Quinn and Manuel were sitting at the kitchen table having breakfast, while watching TV. Carlos set another plate of pancakes on the table, while handing Bre a cup of coffee. He then motioned to the TV. Bre listened changing from one channel to another. She heard the big headlines: Area Man and Wife Arrested for Sex Trafficking. She saw the outside of Ben's house. Walking to the window she looked out. Reporters were camped out with cameras.

"Why are they there? There is no one there. They're in jail."

Quinn's head jerked in the direction of the house. "It's news. It'll take a few days before they leave. In the meantime, anyone who leaves their house will be put on camera. Did you consider that?"

Of course, she hadn't. Glancing at Carlo she raised her eyebrows; who raised his back. It would take a few days before she wanted to slip out. Her face on the nightly news wasn't what she wanted. She glanced at Quinn and Manuel. They needed to stay hidden from the cameras, too.

"Are you guys able to stay here a few days, until the reporters leave?"

 Manuel spoke first, "We are able to send most of our reports from here. I wouldn't want to make it obvious that this was the house of operation either."

The uneasiness filled Bre's stomach again. She reached for the phone and called Bethany.

"I saw the report. I've been trying to call you!"

Bre realized she had her phone off. "Sorry, it's been a long night. I apparently wanted to make sure I wasn't interrupted while I slept." She began to fill Bethany in on all the details. Suddenly tired and not wanting to talk about it any longer, she asked Bethany if she would call Charli;, or better yet, run over to see her. "It may be a few days before I can get out. There are reporters out front." Bethany answered affirmatively, and Bre hung up.

She ate a few bites and whispered to Carlos that she was going back to bed. She hadn't slept well.

He pulled her to him. "Let your mind rest, Bre. That's as important as anything." She nodded, walked up the stairs, and fell into bed. She awoke several hours later feeling more rested and ready to face the day.

The days passed slowly. After three days the reporters realized there was no one around and began to pack up. Waiting another day and leaving early before day break, Quinn and Manuel slipped out first. Bre and Carlos drove out twenty minutes later. It was the first time Bre was actually glad to see the airport. Barely arriving in time, they boarded first class and slept the short flight home.

Back home, Bre called Michael. "Have you heard anything?"

Michael answered, "They have them red handed, even the camera and video. There's no getting out of this!"

Bre wished she felt better. The uneasiness was growing. "How long will this drag out Michael?"

Michael said, "They're up for arraignment on Monday. I'm surprised it's taking this long, but their attorneys are hassling over the FBI's right to burst in as they did."

"God! What right! They were practicing sex slavery." Bre felt her anger rising.

Michael could picture his sister's face.

Smiling he said, "Everything's in order."

Bre asked, "Will their attorney try for a plea bargain? They won't get off on that will they?" The thought caused Bre to rise and begin walking.

"No!" Michael was quick to answer, "The sentence might be shortened but they will get plenty of time."

Bre tried to relax but, still the uneasiness was there. "Keep me informed, will you?"

"Of course." Michael rang off.

Unable to rest, Bre called Carlos to say she was running down to see her mom. "I might call Bethany to see if she'd like to go too." Dialing Bethany, the phone rang and rang. Thinking that's unusual, she called her office. "She hasn't been in today but left a voice message that she would be out of town for a few days." Wondering if she was with Charlie, she left town to drive down.

Arriving early afternoon, she drove by the restaurant to make sure it was closed, and then on to her Mom's. Arriving, she parked in front as she knew they weren't expecting her. As she approached the front, the door swung open. Charlie and Daniel both stepped out.

"This is a nice surprise." Charlie opened her arms.

"Would you like me to move around back or is Bethany's car there?"

Charlie and Daniel glanced at one another. "Was Bethany supposed to be here?"

Bre studied their faces. "Well, I just assumed she was here. Her office said she was out of town for a few days." She glanced around then back to Charlie. "I wasn't able to reach her. Her phone rang and rang, which is really unusual. No voice message nothing."

Charlie's face looked alarmed. Daniel automatically slipped his arm around her. "I'm sure she's fine." But even his voice sounded hollow. Bre walked back to the car and drove around back. Getting out of the car, she remembered Bethany was supposed to visit with them a few days earlier, per her request. As she walked in she asked them, "Did Bethany come by earlier this week? I asked her to, in order to inform you of everything that had happened."

"Oh yes, she came by early and said she was told to fill us in on all the details, which she did. She spent the majority of the day and left at dusk. We tried to talk her into staying, but she said she had rearranged her schedule to come and would be pretty busy the next few days.

"What day was that?" Bre asked.

Daniel spoke first. "It was Monday. I told your mom to stay home and I went in, after visiting with her an hour or so."

Bre glanced at her watch. Her office would be closed now. There was no way she could call to make sure she was back on Tuesday. Anna, her secretary said her voice mail said she'd be gone a few days but when was the first day she was gone? The uneasiness reached a new height and her stomach rolled.   A quick glance at her mom revealed she was feeling the same. Her face paled. Bre reached for her hand. "I'm sure she's fine. She's a very smart lady." But the evening was ruined. They talked over every detail of how Quinn and Manuel observed Ben; the parade of cars filled with officers, the surrounding of the house, and what she had observed. Her voice broke and both Charlie and Daniel reached for her.

"I'll just be glad when it's over, I've had this uneasiness ever since this has gone down. I don't want to regret we did this." Bre began to cry. All that had taken place began to be apparent.

Charlie glanced at Daniel. "Get something hot that will relax her." Daniel nodded and left the room, returning a few minutes later with a china cup full of a warm gold liquid. Bre took a sip and tasted alcohol.

"What is this?" Daniel smiled.

"Something that will relieve the anxiety and cause you to relax." That was enough of an answer for Bre. Though not a drinker she was glad to accept the drink.

He was right. The cup wasn't finished when a warm relaxed feeling filled her.

"Thank you. I needed this."

Daniel smiled. "There's more, if you'd like one before bed."

Although Bre hadn't considered spending the night, she realized she didn't want to drive home either. Daniel excused himself to prepare dinner. "I don't want to be a bother."

Charlie laughed. "Child, you are never a bother. It's leftovers from last night, but there's plenty," and plenty there was. After a dinner of pot roast, potatoes, and salad she helped clean the kitchen. She then took a hot shower. Coming out of the bathroom on her way to the bedroom, Charlie handed her another cup of the golden liquid. "Take it so you can sleep." Bre kissed her, taking the cup. She sipped it, then fell into a deep sleep. Waking early the next morning she realized it was the first good night's sleep she'd had in weeks.

A quick breakfast and she left Charlie, telling her she'd call as soon as she'd talked to Bethany. The drive back was peaceful until she was pulling into the city limits, then the anxiety began to surface. "No, you're fine." She spoke out loud and reached for the stereo to turn on some instrumental music. She'd swung by Bethany's office, noticing her car wasn't in her parking spot. Entering her sister's office, she smiled at Anna. "I know she's out of town, but when did she leave?"

Anna glanced at the office schedule. "She took off Monday and said she had to run out of town and would be back the next day." She made it in on Tuesday and worked late. I know because I left at six. When I came in Wednesday she was already here. I asked her if she went home and she laughed.

"Do I have on the same clothes?"

It was apparent she'd gone home. She left around two and said she was meeting you at your brother's office, Michael - is that his name?"

Bre reached for the desk corner to steady herself. "She hasn't been back since?" Anna gently shook her head no. "She left a message on her office phone saying she would be out of town for a few days."

Bre not wanting to alarm Anna, smiled and thanked her. The minute she was out of the office, she was dialing Michael. As soon as he answered the phone, she asked if he'd heard from Bethany.

"No, was I supposed to?" Bre felt fear leap so raw she was unable to speak. "Bre?"

After a minute Bre answered softly trying to pace herself so she didn't start screaming. "Michael, I have cause to believe something has happened to Bethany. Can I meet with you? Do you have any free time?" By the time she had finished, her voice was shaking and she was fighting back tears.

Michael recognized the panic. His concern shifted at the moment, for Bre "We can do lunch." Bre knew she was in no mood for food.

"Can we meet at your office?"
I'll call Carlos to meet us, too. If you need to you can order in. Nothing for me please."

Michael answered, "Come now, Bre." As she hung up the phone the tears began to fall. "Stop it! This isn't helping" She scolded herself until she managed to take a deep breath; then called Carlos; asking him to meet her at Michael's office.

"What's wrong?" Carlos knew immediately.

"I'll tell you at Michaels."

Though the drive was a short distance, traffic took her longer than she expected. Arriving, she was sent directly in. Michael rose when she walked in. For a few minutes she stood perfectly still, saying nothing. Michael watched his sister. Finally, walking around his desk he reached for her. Bre barely whispered, "Something has happened to Bethany. She's not answering her phone, and she's not at her office. Anna says she left a voice message saying she would be out of town for a few days. "Something is wrong Michael. I feel it. I know it." Michael held her. His first inclination was to begin reassuring her but he felt checked. As he glanced up, Carlos walked in.

One look at Bre's face and Carlos was questioning. "What's wrong? Bre, what's wrong?" Bre turned from Michael to Carlos' arms.

Michael said, "Bre is convinced something has happened to Bethany. We need to sit down and put our heads together."

Carlos gently moved Bre to a chair, and slowly the story began to unfold. "Has there been any demand for money? Any demand of any kind?"

Bre shook her head. "I've had an uneasy feeling since Ben went down. I haven't been able to shake it."

Michael's face was solemn. He reached for a note pad. "Have you been to her apartment before?"

Bre nodded yes. "A few times."

"Do you know the manager?"

Bre answered, "No. I've had no need to."

Michael began to write. "So exactly how long has she been gone?"

"Anna said she left work around two on Wednesday saying she was meeting me at your office."

Michael spoke slowly. "Today is Friday." Hesitating, he spoke. "We need to go to her apartment and talk with the manager to see if he'll let us in. If not, I'll have to see if I can contact Judge Bruce." Michael stood and Bre did also.

"Can we go now?" Michael nodded. "Yes. That's the idea."

Arriving at The Villas, Michael spoke to the manager, who as Michael suspected, was reluctant to allow them entrance. Michael walked away to call and Bre moved quickly, in hopes to persuade the manager.

No one knows for sure, but as the tears began to fall, the manager had a change of heart. "I'm just doing this because you're her sister, and Michael is the Prosecutor." He motioned her to follow. Carlos whistled to Michael, who quickly ended his conversation.

Bethany's apartment was totally in order. Nothing showed any sign of struggle. They listened to the message machine. Bre heard her messages, but there was nothing out of order. "Her car isn't here." Bre turned to Michael.

He reached for his cell phone. "What kind is it?" As Michael spoke into the phone,

Bre turned to Carlos, "Something's wrong. I just feel it." Carlos held her, saying nothing.

He then turned to Bre. "It would be nice if the gifts you and your mother spoke about having, would begin to work about now."

Bre studied his face. He was right. Now was the time they needed to work, but she had never been able to turn them on and off. Bethany also had the gifts. Was it possible to detect where she was at? She reached for her phone and called her mom. When she answered, she said, "Mom, something has happened to Bethany. She's been gone several days. When she left work, she told her secretary she was meeting me at Michael's. She never showed up. Mom, we never made the call for her to meet us. She's been gone two days. Her apartment is fine, but her car is missing." We need the gifts to start working, Mom, and we need it now!"

Chapter 16

The waves lapped against the boat, causing it to sway lightly. Bethany glanced at the man across the room and stirred restlessly. He glanced in her direction. "Do you need to use the lady's room?"

Bethany stood. "Yes, please." she needed to move. Sitting here for days now, was affecting her. How many days had it been, and why hadn't someone come? They have to know I'm missing by now. Trying to keep herself calm had become her hourly goal. Back in the cabin she stood, asking quietly if she could just stand for a while.

Her blonde headed jailer nodded. "It will be dark soon. If you're good we can go for a walk so you can get some exercise." Bethany nodded her thanks with a smile. The blonde jailer, as she had begun to think of him, was much nicer than the red headed one. It was obvious he wouldn't think twice of harming you and would probably take pleasure in it. She shuddered. He had left an hour ago. They were doing twelve-hour shifts – 7:00 to 7:00. She was grateful to have the kinder one during the night. She would hate to think what the other would have done, if he was here.

Thinking back over the last few days, she slowly shook her head. She never saw it coming. Receiving the call asking if she could meet Bre at Michael's office came as a surprise, but with all that was going on with their biological father, it didn't seem worth questioning. She had arranged an appointment for the next day, spoke to her receptionist and left. She was so focused on the meeting with Bre, she hadn't noticed the man standing by her office door, as she exited. It wasn't until she felt someone's arm slip around her waist, and the pressure of the gun under her purse against her side, that she realized what was happening.

She had slid into a car parked ahead of hers. Another man sat behind the wheel.

"Get the keys to her car." She didn't have time to retrieve them. The man beside her had them and tossed them to the man in the passenger seat. He left the car, and as they pulled away, she caught a glimpse of her car following. For a moment she was in shock, not thinking or moving. Then as the reality hit her, she began to fight. It didn't take but a few minutes before she was left gasping for breath.

"Keep messing with me and you will regret it. I don't care if they want you alive or not."

Bethany remembered the drive; the dock, and the boat. Waiting until no one seemed to be around she was then walked quickly to a larger boat docked some distance away. Once inside, she was told calmly and clearly that she was a captive. For how long they didn't know, but, if she was smart, she would make it easy on herself and behave. That was two days ago and though she was allowed to shower, and sleep in a bed, she was always accompanied by one of the two that were her jailers.

Her blonde-haired man who spent the night, motioned for her to take a seat, then walked over to the kitchen and began to make sandwiches and opened a can of soup. She asked if she could help. He glanced at her, motioning to the table. "You can set the table." Bethany stood glad to be able to move. The meal was eaten in silence. Bethany seldom lifted her eyes but occasionally she would see her captor studying her. She hated to think what he was thinking. By the time things were picked up it was dark.

"Grab a jacket. It may get cool." Bethany glanced at the couch where a man's jacket lay.

As she slipped it on, she asked, "Is this yours or the other man's?"

A smile started to play on her captor's lips. "It's mine. If it wasn't, would you take it off?" Bethany's eyes met the blonde man's, as she nodded yes. He said nothing but smiled and nodded.

The breeze felt like heaven. She was so tired of sitting in the cabin. Taking a deep breath, she said softly, "Thank you." Then before she changed her mind she said, "I know you can't give me your real name, but could you make up a first name so…" Her voice trailed off. What did she think they could discuss; the weather; how stupid. She walked along scorning herself when the blonde captor said,

"Jim. Call me Jim. It's not my name, but you can call me that."

Bethany turned to look at him. "Thank you, Jim. This is difficult enough…" Again, her voice trailed off. Jim said nothing - just continued to walk beside her.

Several hours later, they returned to the boat but instead of going in, he motioned her to the top where several chairs sat. As they sat feeling the boat swaying from one side to the other,

Jim asked his first question. "How'd you ever get on the wrong side of these people?"

Bethany glanced at him. "I have no idea who these people are. I think they have the wrong person."

Jim slowly shook his head. "Not this kind, they don't make mistakes. There is something about you something you know, someone you know something."

Bethany could barely breath. "Isn't it possible that for once they are wrong?"

Jim glanced at her. "I'd like to think so, but I don't." With that he stood waiting for her then followed her down. As she entered the cabin, he motioned her toward the bedroom. "Hopefully, you'll rest better tonight."

Bethany smiled slightly. "Thank you, I really appreciated it," and retired for the night.

Stella studied Nickolas. "You're keeping them followed. I don't want any slipups. If there are, you will pay the price."

Nickolas knew she wasn't kidding. "There will be no slipups." He was being extra careful. Bethany's capture had been a piece of cake, but they knew by now she was missing. He had them followed to her apartment building, searching for clues to her whereabouts. He knew Michael well enough to know he'd turn every rock over if he had to, so he had to be very careful. Still he didn't know what Stella's plan was. He took the chance and asked her what her intentions were.

Stella's eyebrows drew together. She glanced out the window. "She's my granddaughter. Are you aware of that?"

Nickolas was. "Yes Ma'am."

Stella turned to look at Nickolas. "They have my son in jail, and if something doesn't happen, he will face prison."

Nickolas tried to follow her thinking, "How is holding Bethany going to help Ben?" Stella stood, coming quickly around the desk. Nickolas wasn't going to sit still. He rose quickly.

Stella said, "It's your stupid fault he's in jail. How could they have gotten the evidence? How could they have known all they knew?" She slapped him, "I ought to have you strung up."

Nickolas spoke calmly, "Ben has been careless the last couple of years. You've said it yourself, to have them brought to his house and to be videoing the..." He let his voice trail off.

Stella swung around to walk over to the window. "If anything happens to my son, he won't be the only one, hurt.'"

Nickolas paused before speaking. "If the law has him evidence and all there's nothing you can do."

Stella turned to look at him before yelling, "I own the law!"

Nicholas gave a shrug. "Apparently not all the law knows that. Keeping Bethany - how does that serve your purpose?"

Stella shook her head in disgust. "The fact that you're even asking that shows how little you've learned. Get out and make sure there's no slipups."

The phone woke Bre early the next morning. Looking at her phone, she sat up. "Yes?" Bre knew her mother wouldn't be calling unless it was important.

"Are you able to come today?"

Bre's mind raced. What did she have scheduled? Without checking, she answered. "Yes. I'll be leaving in an hour."

"Bre," Charlie hesitated, "bring Michael."

Bre hung up and called Michael, who explained he had appointments. "Cancel them, Michael. This is important. I can feel it." Michael said nothing for a minute, then said, "I'll pick you up in an hour. Are you calling Carlos too?"

Bre answered, "Right now." A quick call to Carlos found him to be up, dressed, and ready to leave then. "Give me forty-five minutes, then come down."

The drive to Charlie's was surprisingly quiet, each lost in their own thoughts. Upon arriving, they drove straight to the house. Charlie walked out and motioned them in. Daniel stood by her.

"Would you like something to drink?" Daniel asked. Bre shook her head no and was followed by the others as well.

"Why did you call, Mom? I know it's important." The question was asked as soon as they sat down.

Charlie looked from one to the other, settling on Bre. "I believe Bethany's held captive on a boat."

Bre sat up straight. "Why do you say that?"

Charlie glanced at Daniel who nodded to her. "I had a vivid dream early this morning. "I saw her in a boat. She was being watched by a blonde man. I know she's on a boat. I saw it clearly."

Carlos turned to Michael. "Do you know if Ben has a boat?"

Michael looked from one to the other. "No, but it won't take much to find out. Let me make a few calls." He rose to walk out of the room. After several minutes, he returned to say, "He does indeed have a boat called 'Cilia's Dream'."

Charlie shook her head. "That's not it. That's not the name on the boat."

Bre looked at her mom. "Did you see the name on the boat?"

Charlie glanced around the room. "It was called 'Stella'."

Bre rose up. "Stella, isn't that Ben's mother's name?"

Charlie nodded yes. Michael grabbed his phone and began calling, as he walked out of the room. No one spoke until Michael came back.

"Grab your belongings, we're moving, and moving fast."

Bre turned to her mom. "Do you want to come?"

Charlie shook her head. "No. Just let me know when you have her!"

The drive back was driven at top speed. Arriving back, Michael was given the news. The police had surrounded the place, all under cover, and had waited until the go ahead was given. The search warrant had been granted and they were beginning to move in. Michael spoke, "You're probably being watched.   Do what you do best."

Bethany had awakened early. She wanted to be up before her captors changed shift. The man with the red hair made her skin crawl. She didn't want to be unprepared when he came. Waking early made for a long day, but at least, if she was up and dressed, she didn't have to be concerned about him walking in on her. She really felt he was capable of anything. Suddenly she was replaying the events of the evening before. It was obvious, the blonde was having second thoughts about being involved in this. His offer to go for a late-night walk was not only out of character for a kidnapper, but he seemed concerned about her well-being. "I wonder how he got here? How did he get involved with people like this?"

Even as she pondered the question, she could hear voices in the next room. Her other captor had arrived. She hurried to finish dressing. Standing by the door, she strained to hear the hushed conversation. Her stomach growled. She'd eaten little in the last few days here and was beginning to feel the effects. She sat on the bunk bed, wondering if she should walk out or sit until her door opened. She felt tired and weak physically; little food; and no exercise was having an effect.

As she pondered if she should stay or join her captors the door opened. "If you're hungry, there's food." She glanced at Red, as she had come to mentally call him. His head jerked toward the kitchen.

Following slowly, she was surprised to see an assortment of breakfast food on the small table. "I thought I'd grab some breakfast and eat before I left for the day." Her eyes met the blonde stranger. She fought to keep from allowing the smile to surface. Unsure of what Red would do, she nodded and thanked him. As she helped herself and began to eat, she wondered why would he not only consider this, but do it? Was he aware she wasn't being fed during the day, only evenings? It appeared so. She ate slowly, savoring every bite and, when offered seconds, accepted.

She asked if she could clean up, but Red responded,

"No, you've eaten. We need to talk. Get back to your room."

Her eyes met the blonde stranger and she managed a smile to thank him. Back in her room her mind raced. What was going on? Why would this stranger go get food, and come back so she could eat? Her mind again wandered. I wonder if we had met under different circumstances, what would have happened. She couldn't understand what he was doing with Red. They were complete opposites.

Sometime later, she heard the cabin door shut. Now she was alone- with Red. She felt her stomach churn. "Stay calm, don't panic" She talked herself down. Sitting on the bed, she wished for something to read, she only found one book that she half read. Unable to concentrate, she was wondering if she dared to lay back to take a nap. It wasn't unusual for Red to leave her alone for several hours before he yanked open her door to demand she come up front so he could, keep an eye on her.

The sudden noise from the front of the cabin caused her heart to jump to her throat. Voices yelling, Hands up! Hands up!" caused her hands to rise as she held her breath. She could hear the rustling, the sounds of several chairs falling, the voices of many men. Then she heard her name being called. She stood, not knowing if she should move or stand still. A knock sounded at her door, and slowly the cabin door moved. She waited until she saw the undercover agent.

"Are you Bethany?" She nodded yes. "You're ok. You're safe now."

Slowly her trembling hands covered her mouth. The silent tears fell. After several minutes passed, she began to quietly laugh.

"How did you know? How did you find me?"

The agent looked at her. "It appears, through a dream."

Bethany's head raised to meet the officer's eyes. "I think I know who the dreamer was." She slowly followed the agent out, feeling like she was in a daze, if not sleep walking through a dream herself.

Michael wheeled the car into the harbor. He saw nothing unusual until he turned the curve and saw, there in the distance, the flashing lights. Bre held Carlos' hand in a vice grip, barely breathing. As they came to a stop, she saw Bethany with agents being escorted from the boat.

A loud sob broke from her, as she scrambled out of the car.

"Bre!" Michael yelled. "Wait!"

Too late, she was rushing to her sister yelling her name. Bethany saw her and stood - her arms opened. Together they stood holding each other, while officers circled, talking with one another.

Michael introduced Carlos and spoke with several agents. Bethany would need to come down to answer questions. Bre asked if she could come also. As they stood discussing what was to follow,

Bre turned to Carlos and handed him her phone. "Would you call Mom? Her number is in my phone.

Tell her we have Bethany and she's safe."

No one noticed the black sedan that eased out of the harbor.

Nickolas had received word of the early morning trip out of town and had joined one of his men. He then trailed Michael to the Harbor. Watching from a distance, he knew better than to return to Stella. He drove to his house, packed quickly, slid several different passports from between his mattress, and headed for a rental car agency. He didn't want his car to be at the airport. Leaving it anywhere but there would buy him time.

    As he left and headed to the airport, he tossed his phone, and grabbed the extra one he had. He always wanted to live someplace other than the good old U.S. of A. Now he had no choice. As he boarded the plane he never looked back.

Chapter 17

Bethany spent most of the evening answering questions. Exhausted, she was released and rode home with Bre. "Tomorrow we'll grab some clothes. You need to spend some time here." Bethany nodded; glad to be someplace safe.

The first week Bethany's sleep was filled with dreams of the boat, her captors, and the rescue, but soon it was on the blonde guard. Where was he? There was no mention of him on the news. Surprisingly, Red had spilled everything. Stella was arrested, before she was able to skip the country, and each day more surfaced from the investigation.

It was impossible to forget it, with the news and the reporters calling for interviews. Bre suggested now would be the right time to take vacation time.

 Bethany agreed, but refused to go anywhere. "I'm not sure I'll ever feel safe again." Bre studied her sister. She couldn't imagine what she must have been feeling during that time of captivity and wished there was something she could do to turn back the clock.

"It will pass, you'll see. Your life will feel secure again." She spoke the words, though not sure she believed them herself.

In the midst of all that was taking place, the wedding was drawing closer. Bre took her mother and Bethany for fittings then on a drive to the country club to show where the event would take place. For the first time, Bre saw Bethany smiling and laughing.

They had stopped watching or listening to the news. "It will take six months to a year, before this goes to trial." Michael shared during lunch at her house. "You're fortunate. The judge has refused bond. That is unheard of in this day and age." Bre smiled glancing at her sister but Bethany's thoughts were remembering the two-hour walk with the blonde captor; who's name no one, including Red. She had shared her information with Michael and Bre, but it was a dead-end trail that seemed to go nowhere. She was shocked at how many times her thoughts turned to him wondering where he was. She shook her head. It would be a face she was not to see again; or so she thought.

The weeks passed and slowly things eased up. The reporters had stopped calling and Bethany returned to work a few hours every other day. As the excitement began to build regarding Bre's wedding, things were slowly returning to normal.

Bethany stepped out of her office. She looked both ways and started towards her car.

"Bethany." She turned toward the voice that sounded so familiar. Still, her hand reached for her purse, and the gun she now carried. There he stood beside a car a few feet away. He half raised his hand, as if not knowing if he should or not. Bethany stood dead still her heart in her throat. Without thinking her one hand reached out as if to ward off. "You don't have to worry. I won't hurt you." Jim, as she knew him took a step forward. "I just wanted to say I'm sorry that I was involved with any of that. It was part of my job."

For the first time since her capture, she felt anger rise up within her. "Your job! Your job!" Her voice raised. Jim slowly backed up a few feet and raised his hand to his lips in a motion to quiet down.

"I wouldn't have let them hurt you. I hadn't been with the organization long." He smiled. "They don't even know my real name."

Bethany looked at him. Slowly the anger drained and in its place was confusion. "Why are you here?"

Jim shrugged his shoulders. "I've just thought of you a lot and was concerned they might try something again."

Bethany took a few steps towards him. "Ben and Stella are in jail and, hopefully will be locked up for a long time."

Jim glanced away. "There's a lot more than Ben and Stella. It just matters, if this was a personal vendetta or the family business."

Bethany looked at this stranger. Why she said what she did was something she was to wonder about in the weeks ahead. "Ben is my father. My twin and I are his illegitimate children."

It was Jim's turn to step back as he looked at Bethany, going over each feature. "Well, I'll be." He shook his head. "Yeah, his mother wouldn't want that to be known and she couldn't have you contesting any inheritance."

He laughed lightly and, after a long moment, said, "I just wanted you to know. I'm glad you're well."

 As he turned to leave Bethany said, "Are you still working for that organization?"

Jim turned back, smiled, and said, "No. I had my own reasons for the short time there. They have no information on me, and I'm not of any importance for them to continue to look for me." As he walked away, he turned once again to say, "Bethany, hopefully, this is more of a personal agenda with Stella so they will have no future agenda with you." With that he took off jogging. Bethany watched him till he was out of sight. Turning to her car, she once again glanced around her before sliding in.

The evening of the rehearsal dinner was a joyful gala. Bethany, still living with Bre, helped her sister through the rehearsal. Everything flowed beautifully. The dinner, also at the Country Club, was decorated beautifully as well, and Carlos family joined in with the festivities. The evening ended with each member of Carlos' family rising to toast the happy couple and to pronounce a blessing upon them. Hours later, Carlos and Bre kissed. "Tomorrow!" was whispered by both.

The honeymoon would be spent in Hawaii. Bethany had stated she would be moving out during that time. Bre was quick to respond. "No. Why don't you consider staying at Carlos'?" Bethany looked as if she was deciding if she should laugh or not.

"Carlos'! Why would I be staying at Carlos'?"

Bethany answered, "Because it will be empty. He will be with me."

Bethany laughed. "I couldn't afford Carlos' place."

Bre pulled her sister to her. "I can, and it would be my joy to have my sister living a few houses down from me."

Bethany stepped back. Looking at her sister, she realized she was serious. "You're serious?"

Bre laughed. "I am! We will work out everything when I'm back." The hour was nearing one in the morning when they fell asleep.

The next morning was full of activities; early brunch; nail technicians worked with one after another in the wedding party; as did the stylist. Arriving early to get individual pictures, Bre took the time to step inside the large room where the ceremony would take place. Pink flowers draped the stage, and pale white shears hung at the back of the platform where Carlos and she would stand to be united as husband and wife. The unity candle was decorated, and as she looked around the lights were lowered, and what looked like a thousand twinkle lights filled the ceiling, silhouetting across the room.

The beauty caused Bre to gasp. It was perfect. She wouldn't have changed a thing. Bethany entered with Carlos' sister, both looked stunning in dresses of different shades of pink. They had decided on a style that was off the shoulders and fell gracefully to the floor.

"Bre, come look at the dining room. It is absolutely stunning." Taking a minute to step inside, Bre understood what she meant.

Michael had spared no cost to see that everything was perfect. Tables and chairs in white with pink bows tied behind each chair. Pink napkins were placed at each china setting and different shades of pink and white flowers decorated each table. The head table glittered with lights and candles throughout. Flowers cascaded across the table.

"It's beautiful!" Bre found she was holding her breath. An usher stepped in to announce that guests were beginning to arrive, and unless they wanted to be seen they needed to retire to the bridal suite.

The minutes ticked by then suddenly, the time was here. As the violin began to play, Bre looked into the eyes of her brother. "I love you so. Thank you for always being there for me. I couldn't have done it without you."

Michael looked at his sister, his fingers gently brushing the tears that threatened to fall. "You have been a joy. I couldn't have chosen a better sister." He glanced around, "I'm sure Mom and Dad are rejoicing."

Bre smiled and as the piano began to play, they began their walk down as everyone stood. Bre smiled as she saw Carlos standing at the altar. His face was beaming. As she stood beside him and began to recite their vows, she knew this was truly the happiest day of her life. As she turned to look at their congregation with the pronouncing of husband and wife her eyes fell on her mother. Glancing quickly at Bethany, then Carlos, she knew her life had truly come full circle.

In the back, a blonde Jim watched it all.

www.ingramcontent.com/pod-product-compliance
Lightning Source LLC
Chambersburg PA
CBHW021332060726
47591CB00006B/1982